THE OLD ONE

P. A. DOUGLAS

To H. P. Lovecraft and the insanity he was able to put down on paper.

Acknowledgements

For this first edition of THE OLD ONE, my thanks go to everyone at Severed Press, Dane Hatchell, Alan M. Clark, Edward Lee, Brian Keene, and Sarah VonKain.

Author's Note

This book is a book of fiction and although it is in homage to H. P. Lovecraft, I took certain liberties with the mythos. Nonetheless, I am sure you will find this a fast paced, fun read.

ONE

There was nothing special about the day leading up to that moment when his stomach ruptured. Blood splashed out around his midsection as the meaty flesh separated, sending bits of entrails and miasma all over the bed in a slopping wet heap of filth.

What spewed from his gut was an utter abomination.

It changed everything.

*****

The day had started much like any of the other countless days for Ryan C. Perish. He was a retired old man that had been laid off from work long ago because of bad bones. The days sitting idle generally bled together. That's what made them countless.

Cool, crisp wind pushed the ocean's whitecaps against the beach and back out to the ocean. The moon set high in a cloudless sky making it unnaturally bright for such a late hour.

The calm before the storm, he thought.

Ryan liked it like that. Cool, calm, and quiet. He was never one to go fishing during the day. Too many problems. The pier was always overcrowded and noisy. Fishing lines got crossed. And the sun was out, which Ryan couldn't stand. At the ripe old age of 68 he couldn't tolerate the direct heat for long periods like he used to.

Topsail Beach, NC, was a small family-oriented seaside island town with pristine stretches of sandy beaches. It pleased Ryan to call it home, having lived there all his life. However, he was getting too old for the scene now. The paper mill was closed and everything had given way to tourism. It no longer mattered. His back was shot. There was no way for him to return to the ways of old even if the mill was still in operation.

Since retirement, he spent most of his time hanging out at the local fishermen's bar sharing stories and drinking whisky. At night, he almost always found himself in his Beavertail Phantom water-fowling kayak. As a water-fowling kayak, the Phantom was specifically built to overcome the challenges often found when hunting out of smooth-bottomed, conventional kayaks. The twin-hull, catamaran-style bottom provided a stable platform to support the additional weight of hunting gear. Hunting wasn't the reason why he owned the boat. He wasn't a hunter. In fact, he didn't even own a gun. He hated firearms with a passion. His younger brother had been killed by a handgun. He didn't like going anywhere near them.

He bought a Beavertail Phantom because of its stability. He could sit and relax, even when the waves were somewhat choppy, and even while tied off under the pier with a rope.

That night the waves were nonexistent. The water was as flat as flat could be. The only occasional sounds were splashes of fish feeding on top-water insects. The smell of sea salt and the gentle breeze eased his internal pains.

Ryan took a deep breath and exhaled a sigh of relief as he leaned back in the kayak to get more comfortable. He had been tied off at the far end of the pier for the last two hours just relaxing and casting his line. He hadn't caught anything yet. Not even a single bite. But it didn't matter. The silence, smell, the full moon, and the view of an endless black were enough for him to enjoy the night.

The stars were bright.

He reached into his coat pocket and pulled out a half empty flask of bourbon. He unscrewed the cap, took a long swig, and sucked air in through his teeth. The spirits burned going down. No matter how much he drank, he could never get used to it. His chest felt warm as the alcohol settled in his stomach. Satisfied, he took one more quick sip, sloshed it around in his mouth, and put the flask back into hiding.

Despite what tourists happening upon him might have thought, Ryan wasn't a town drunk that spent most of his nights fishing. Sure, he fished a lot, but he wasn't a drunk. He drank, but wasn't the stereotypical overbearing bum. He had his own place on the edge of town, and like all of his possessions, it was paid for. He had enough money saved up from working at the mill to not burden anyone. At least he felt like he wasn't a burden on anyone. He sure as hell hoped he wasn't. Sure, Trent and Tina, his neighbors, helped him with his grocery shopping, but that wasn't because he was feeble. It wasn't like he needed help getting in and out of the shower or cleaning house. He just didn't like to shop alone. Heather had always been the one to do that. However, just like the old paper mill, she went before her time.

Ryan missed her deeply. Everything about her. Her scent. Her sweet endearing laugh. The way one dimple formed on the left side of her cheek when she smiled.

If there was any one thing worse than guns, it was cancer.

Cancer had taken his wife.

Ryan smiled. A lone tear fell from his right eye. It wasn't from sadness or loneliness. No, he wasn't one to suffer from much of that. His tear was shed out of joy. He had loved Heather more than anything in the world. Despite the hand he had been dealt in life, he was thankful that his mind was still in working order, unlike some of the others his age back at the bar. At least, he was lucky enough to recall the memories of the life that he and Heather shared. Seeing her image in his mind, it was as if she were sitting in the kayak with him. The cool ocean draft lightly blew across his neck and tickled the hairs on his skin. For a moment, it reminded him of her tender touch.

That was one of the main reasons he fished so much. It always made him think of her.

The fishing rod suddenly jerked in his hand, breaking him from the spell of the past.

He had a bite.

"Got you now," he whispered.

He tightened his grip on the rod and scanned the dark trying to locate the end of the line. His eyes weren't what they used to be. The line tugged again and he found what he was looking for. The small red and white float dunked under the water and then resurfaced.

He smiled.

"Looks like another lucky night, Heather." He yanked the rod a few times to set the hook and watched the water.

The reel began to unwind, sounding like a bug in distress. He hoped he snagged a big one. Another hard yank locked the reel.

"The Big kings must still be in." He heaved, testing the resolve of his catch.

If it was a Big king, then there was about to be a bit of a fight. The largest one he had ever caught was 48 pounds. Ryan had spent most of the week bottom fishing. VA mullet hit best on bloodworms, but he managed to catch a few spots, some puppy drum, flounder, and trout during the week, but that was it. The overall conditions for fishing had started to improve with the cooler weather starting to come in.

Ryan tugged.

The catch tugged back. The fight began.

He stood in the kayak as he had done countless times before. The wide berth the small boat provided kept it from tipping over. In truth, he wasn't even sure why it was called a kayak. It really didn't even look like one to him. He craned his head to the right, checking the rope's knot he had tied to the pier. It was still tight. Satisfied, he tugged hard, lifting the fishing pole up over his head, reeling it in with everything he had. Each breath he took strained against his brittle old lungs.

Come on, old man. You got this, he thought. He leaned forward to give the rod and fishing line some slack for a second and then pulled back to gain the advantage. *We ain't lettin' this one get away.* His arm muscles, despite their old age, tightened. Veins bulged in his neck. There wasn't much of the fishing line left. Whatever he had on the other end of that hook wasn't much below the surface.

Even though he was expecting it, Ryan jumped with a twinge of fright when the fish broke the water's surface.. Water splashed across his legs and into the boat. The Big king's head flailed violently against the hook as he tried to pull it in.

"Dang... you sure are a big'n," Ryan said, trying to catch his breath.

The fish's scales glistened against the moonlight as it slid over the kayak's side and flopped into the boat. Ryan sat down to rest, setting the rod in its holster to free his hands to keep the large fish from flopping out.

"Eh, gross," he cringed. The hook was stuck out of the fish's eye.

Blood and salt water seeped from the opening.

Ryan loved fishing. Didn't mind the smell. Didn't mind the sticky fingers from handling the live bait. But this was a little much. Removing the hook was the part he never got used to. He never was one for scaling and cleaning. He always just put his catch on ice and got the local butcher to deal with it the next morning. So what if it cost a couple bucks. To him, any money was worth not having to stick his hands down the damn thing's mouth and yank out entrails.

Ick...

Now, he knew better than to roll his eyes and play fingertip tug with the hook when he was around some of the other roughnecks that fished. If any of them caught wind of it, he knew good and well that it would spread like wildfire back at the bar. It didn't matter. It was late. No one was around. At least, he thought no one was around. He took one reassuring glance to either side anyway, feeling silly. Unless, Earl Harper, one of his buddies from the bar, could walk on water and didn't have to be at work in the morning, there was no reason to think anyone would see him playing skittish with the fishing hook.

He might have been a little silly about the gore, but Ryan wasn't dumb. With his left hand still holding the flailing fish to the floor of the kayak, he reached into his pants pocket and retrieved his pocket knife.

"Sorry 'bout this, pal," Ryan said, stabbing the fish in the area where its heart should have been, "but I don't need to get my hand hooked. No, sir. That wouldn't be any good."

Ryan waited a moment. The fish's squirming subsided to nothing more than labored gasps for air.

Nearby, he heard a bird's wings flap overhead. Probably taking perch at the top of the pier waiting for scraps. That was another one of the reasons Ryan hated fishing during the day. The birds were out of control. It would never fail. Someone always got shit on by those stupid rats with wings. Between the kids feeding the damn things and the idiots that felt the need to gut their fish right then and there, the birds overran the place. The dumb thing was probably on the railing overhead waiting for a hand out. If there was anything worse than the birds, it was a bum, and these birds were both.

He didn't bother looking up. With his right hand applying pressure, the knife still lodged in the thing's head, he reached for the hook with his free hand.

"Let's get this over with." Ryan gritted his teeth and grasped the cold wet hook between two fingers. "Got to admit though, good catch. Don't you think, Heather?"

Just pull the damn thing out, he thought, as if it were his Heather telling him somehow. He knew better. Old habits were hard to break, and talking to her wasn't one he was looking to be giving up.

Ryan closed his eyes and took a deep breath.

He pulled hard on the hook. There was no point in trying to pry the hook out, leaving the fish's flap trap intact. When he took it in to be cleaned, they were going to chop the head off anyway. The sound of flesh tearing reached his ears. When he looked down, the hook was in hand. The dead creature's maw had been nearly torn clean off. Chunks of skin and meat dangled from the hook. Blood smearing his thumb and pointer finger made him instinctively reach over into the water to rinse his hand before setting the hook aside.

Ryan's scream was cut short. A watery splash took its place.

Something grabbed his hand from within the drink. He was overboard and in the water before he realized what the hell was happening.

The cold rushed over his body as his mind struggled to realize he had been pulled from the boat.

He gasped for air. It felt like two hands squeezed each of his lungs as tightly as they could. His mind swirled and his eyes burned against the salty blackness. He fought against the water around him, trying to decide which way was up. Both of his hands were free and whatever had pulled him in wasn't there now.

Panic set in.

Whatever it was, it was probably still close by. His heart raced. It pounded against his chest with a fierce trembling, and hurt just as badly as his lungs did.

His mind went white. Heather was there standing before him. She was wearing a long, flowing white robe. Against the white around her, it was almost hard to make out anything else but her face, hands, and feet. She glistened like an angel full of light and pure love. His heart swelled with peace, despite the situation, despite whatever the hell had pulled him from the boat. He reached out trying to take her hand. Embrace the light. Finally be with her for eternity. God, he wanted that more than anything. To finally be able to hold her in his arms after all those years alone. He tried to tell her he loved her and missed her. Wished she was still with him. But he couldn't talk. She reached up, putting a cold finger on his lips. It felt coarse and slimy. No matter. It was good to feel her touch after all that time. She told him it was going to be okay. His time wasn't over yet. She had a bigger purpose for him. She needed him to live. There were other things to do. She reached out, pulling him into her and she kissed him on the lips. Ryan felt a tear form in the corner of his eye despite the fact that he knew he was still under water. Something slammed violently in the back of his throat and went down hard. He felt sick. The reality that he couldn't breathe was finally setting in. His stomach churned, and then Heather's beautiful face changed into something hideous. Then, just like that, she was gone. The blackness and his stinging eyes returned. Just when his limbs were about to go limp and his mind wavering into a darker place, Ryan felt the ocean floor at his feet.

He kicked against it as hard as he could and rushed to the water's surface.

He broke to the surface and gasped for air. Waves of numbing coldness washed over his entire body. Pain flooded his lungs, as if the air entering was unexpected.

*****

Ryan lunged forward, somehow sitting up in bed. Had it all been a bad dream?

His mind was clouded and confused. Whose bed was he lying in? He had never seen this room before in his life. The clothes he had been wearing were folded neatly on a nightstand next to him. They were pressed and dry. That was when he realized he wasn't wearing anything. He lifted the blanket and found that he was bare down to his skivvies. Hoping for the slightest hint as to where he was, he took in the room. A photo on the wall. A familiar friend sitting in a chair. There was nothing. The room was empty. Just him, the nightstand, and the bed. A small wooden Crucifix hung on the wall above the bed. That was it.

He remembered the fishhook and falling in the water. Or did he get pulled in? He remembered seeing his love, Heather. She had said something to him, but he couldn't remember what it was. It was important. That much he knew.

"Hell…ooo?" Ryan called out, his throat hoarse. "Hello? Is someone there?"

"He's awake," someone called out from another room.

A moment later, the last person Ryan expected to see stepped into view.

"Hey, Perish," Paul Stellie said, stepping in the doorway with a wide smile.

"Hey, buddy," Ryan replied, clearing his still sore throat.

Paul was about 19 years old. Great kid, a bag boy at the local farmers market on the other side of town. Pretty much everybody knew everybody on the island. Like most teenagers, he was going through phases. But that was nothing. He worked hard, played hard, and rarely got into trouble. Ryan had known him since he was just a small pup. It had always amazed the old man to watch him growing into the young adult he was. They would chat it up at the farmer's market on the occasions Paul had helped him with his groceries to the car.

Paul was into something called the Facebook, or the Bookface. Ryan wasn't sure. Maybe it was some new band the kids were into these days. Other than that, he was currently saving most of the money he made from being a bagboy for a set of wheels. The way Paul put it, *'I'm never going to get a girlfriend being driven around by my mom all the time.'* They both laughed about that, because it was true. Ryan enjoyed their chats. Beyond the small talk, it never went anywhere else. But that was to be expected. What teenager wanted to be seen being friends with an old lonely man like Ryan?

Paul's mom, Rose Stellie, was a widow. Unlike cancer that had taken his Heather away, Mr. Stellie had been taken from this life by a drunk driver a few years back. Surprisingly, Paul and his mother had taken it a lot better than the rest of town had expected them to. Ryan wasn't sure what she did for a living. Other than being a little on the sad side, she was a really kindhearted lady.

"Had us scared, man. Glad to see you came around." Paul grinned, rubbing the stubble on his young chin.

"Where are we?" He knew it was silly to ask. They were at Paul's house. That was the logical answer, but when he opened his mouth that was what came out.

"My casa-su-casa. You're in the spare bedroom," Rose Stellie said, stepping past Paul with a glass of water. "Here—drink this."

"Thanks," Ryan said, sitting back against the headboard and looking down to make sure he was covered up. He took a big gulp from the glass and asked, "What happened?"

"Dude, I'll tell you what happened," Paul responded, his voice high pitched with excitement. "You almost died. That's what. Me and Chels…" He cleared his throat and started over, his mom glaring at him. "I mean Chad and me were walking up and down the beach. Just when we were about to head up onto the pierr, I heard something splash in the water. That was when I spotted your boat tied off at the far end."

Ryan's mind flashed to the moment when his hand went into the water.

"But you weren't on the boat," Rose spoke up. "You were lucky, Mr. Perish. Had Paul and Chelsea," she rolled her eyes at her son, "not been there, you would have drowned."

"Yeah, dude." Paul smiled, his shoulders straight with pride. "Once I got to the shoreline, Bro, you popped up gasping for air. I jumped in after you, dude. Good thing the tide wasn't in. I don't know that I would'a been able to pull you in by myself."

"Thanks, Paul." Ryan nodded, and then looked down at the folded clothing on the nightstand. "How long have—"

"You were out for nearly a whole day," Rose said, cutting him off. "It's seven o'clock and the sun's already gone down. I'm sure you could use something to eat. How does something light sound?"

"That would be great," Ryan said, taking another sip from his glass of water.

Rose nodded and turned away leaving Paul and Ryan to themselves.

"She'll be back in a second," the teenager explained. "We had some soup already on the stove."

"That's nice." Ryan smiled, ignoring the tense feeling in his stomach. "So, who is this Chelsea girl? I thought you weren't having any luck with the ladies, what with not having a car to call your own."

"Yeah. Well, uh," Paul said, flustered. Running his fingers through his sandy-brown hair, he said, "Well, my mom don't much care for her. But what does she know? I think she…"

Ryan tried listening to the boy as he talked about this girl—obviously smitten. But he couldn't focus. His stomach started cramping and felt as if it was going to burst at the seams at any moment. Something was wrong. It was almost as if he was experiencing a severe kidney infection. He grabbed at his side trying to breathe. He stretched in the bed trying to make the pain go away, but it was only getting worse. The pain rapidly grew so harsh his vision started to blur.

"I…" That was the last word Ryan C. Perish had the chance to utter.

His body convulsed in a fit of agony.

"Oh, my God!" Rose shouted, stepping into the room and nearly dropping the bowl of soup that was in her hand. Setting it on the nightstand, she shouted at Paul to go call for help.

Before Paul could turn around and make his way out of the room, Ryan's midsection exploded. With a painful gurgling grunt, his stomach ruptured in a firework display of red and white. Blood sprayed across his body and all over the bed. His intestines slapped wet in his lap. Blood ran down his chin from his open mouth, his eyes soulless and vacant. Chunks of meat splashed across the wall, bits of it falling to the floor.

Rose screamed.

Ryan C. Perish was dead.

The tentacle-like things that squirmed out from inside the old man's corpse were on Rose and her son before either of them could comprehend what was happening.

TWO

Max Willgood smiled, poking his head past the blinds of the window in his den.

"Looks like it's gonna start raining soon," he said, looking out toward his neighbor's house.

"What'd the weather channel say, dear?" his wife Hanna asked, from behind her needlepoint project.

"Not sure. Didn't catch the weather today," he replied, not taking his eyes away from the window.

The sky outside started to grow bleaker by the minute. He was right. Thick and menacing clouds rolled in. A faint grumble of thunder echoed off in the distance, followed by a sudden flash of bright white.

"Hmmm…" He shook his head. "When it rains, it pours."

"Would you get away from that window already?" Hanna insisted. "You're making me anxious. It's the first day of vacation and you're already restless. Now, come sit down. Let's find something to watch on TV."

"I'm not the one who wanted to take vacation," Max muttered. "I would'a been just fine with a payout. We could use the money."

Hanna didn't say anything. She never did. She just shrugged and went back to her embroidery. They had been married for well over ten years now, and knew each other inside and out. Most people married for that length of time thought it was cool to finish one another's sentences. Hell, they could finish each other's thoughts. They could just look at one another and know what they were going to say. When they first moved to Topsail Beach about 5 years ago, Max had gotten a job as an auto mechanic at one of the local shops. He loved working with his hands, so he enjoyed the job. It had actually been Hanna's idea for them to make the move. The economy had been pretty rough up north and they both hated the cold weather. Since Max was naturally high strung, Topsail Beach seemed like the perfect place to relocate. Stress-free living was what they needed. Small, family oriented. Everybody knew everybody. They liked that quality. Before they actually committed to the move, Max managed to lock the job at the local repair shop, *Don's Automotive*. Because of that, the deal was sealed. Wasn't the greatest in pay, but it worked. Having been married early on at the ripe old age of 19, both he and Hanna were only 29, going on 30. Hanna was the one closer to 30 by about two months, but if you had asked, she would deny it. She was currently between jobs, which was why Max would have preferred the check to the days off. But, with the use it or lose it policy in effect, he took it. He didn't like it. He didn't like sitting idle and he knew Hanna could tell. Being at home all day was eating at him. She just smiled and shook her head some more, and then went back to threading her needle.

A loud roar grumbled outside suggesting the rain would soon fall.

"Looks like it's about to start getting pretty nasty." Max stepped away from the window, scratched the thick mustache under his bulbous nose and sat down in his recliner next to Hanna. "And no… I don't plan on shaving it any time soon, dear."

"But I don't like it," she said, rolling her eyes at him. "It tickles my face when we kiss."

"You're just going to have to get used to it," Max said, licking at the mustache with his lips. He grabbed the remote to the TV and turned it on. Finding the weather channel, he nodded. "You know good and well that if I'm to be the best mechanic this side of the island I need to look the part."

She chuckled.

He definitely looked the part. Too well in fact.

His scruffy jet black hair was short and somehow always a mess. His monster of a mustache just as thick, and just as dark, aside for the one small patch of gray hairs under his left nostril. When the discolored hairs first started to show, Hanna insisted he not pluck them out, because it gave him character. He thought it was silly, but kept them anyway. Hanna hated his mustache and if there was one thing she *did* like about it, he sure as hell wasn't going to get rid of that.

"So, what's this one going to be?" Max leaned up from his chair trying to sneak a peek at Hanna's needle point.

She pulled it up to keep him from seeing it. "You know you can't look until I'm finished."

When they first bought the house, they came across tons of yarn and unfinished yarn art pieces in the attic. They must have been left by the previous owners. Hanna had never been into needlepoint before then, but instantly fell in love with it. Surprisingly she had a knack for it. Before long, she was spitting out a new piece every couple of weeks. The wall that the flat screen television set hung on was lined from one end to the other with pieces she had completed. Mushroom embroideries, houses, owls, cats, all of them hand embroidered with care. She was actually getting really good at it. Before long, there wouldn't be any more room on that wall for her creations and her art would be encroaching on the other wall space that had been designated for family photos.

Max didn't mind. It made her happy and she really did seem to enjoy it.

He thumbed the volume on the remote, the commercials finally giving way to the weather.

"The hurricane season has officially kicked off. It's going to be another active season with Tropical storm Faye stirring up trouble in the Atlantic off the coast of North Carolina." The weatherman on TV was saying. "Last year's season had 19 named storms, 10 category 1 hurricanes and 1 major category 4 hurricane. From 1995 to 2011, the Atlantic has averaged 15 named storms, 8 hurricanes and 4 major hurricanes. This is not to be taken lightly and preperations have been taken as local citizens are gearing up for another bumpy year. With maximum sustained winds suggested to reach up to 70 mph when Faye reaches landfall, the Tropical storm could very well develop into a hurricane by daybreak. It is, however, expected to reduce its…"

"Preperations?" Max scoffed, drowning the television out. "I didn't even know we had a storm headed this way. Did you?"

"Nope." Hanna smiled, her pearly whites just above the embroidery she was working on. "I thought I heard Becky talking to someone about the weather when I stopped by the store to get some milk and eggs this morning. But I didn't notice anybody rushing to get supplies or anything."

"Hmm…" Max shrugged. "That's crazy. Hopefully, it doesn't turn out to be a big one. Remember last year when the bridge going out of Surf City got flooded out? That sucked."

"Yep," Hanna agreed, her hands still steady at work on the yarn art.

The island only had one way to the mainland other than by boat. That was to drive all the way through Surf City on the other side of town and hit the bridge off the island. It never failed. When there was an evacuation, you could forget trying the bridge. It was always congested as hell. If it did get bad Max already knew it was pointless to try the bridge. Boat would be the only way to go. Thing was, he didn't have access to a boat. That, at times, stressed him out a little, especially this time of year. But he refused to let on regardless if Hanna knew he felt that way or not.

"You think we should go to the store and stock up on stuff just in case?"

"It wouldn't hurt." Hanna set the embroidery aside, and then stood to her feet. "I'm going to go get something to drink. You want anything?"

Max nodded.

Just when she was about to step out of the room and into the kitchen, she turned back and said, "And no peeking!"

Max laughed as she stepped out of the room. Sure enough, he snuck a glance at what she had been working on for well over a week. It was embroidery of some of the characters from *The Muppets*. The only one he recognized was the frog and the one named Miss Piggy.

"You better not be peeking!" Max heard Hanna call out from the kitchen.

It made him smile.

Sitting there waiting on his wife to return, he started flipping the channels to find a movie for the two of them to watch. When he listened close enough, he could hear the faint sound of rain outside. It had already started coming down.

Gonna be another great hurricane season, he thought. *Always got to trade one bad thing for another. Guess the rain is better than the snow.*

Max was startled by a sudden crash outside. At first, he brushed it off as being caused by the storm getting closer, but it didn't sound like thunder. It sounded more like something was out in the yard. He turned down the television and sat there for a second listening. He could hear the rain beating against the roof. It was coming down harder than he thought. Thunder bellowed out in a low drone and faded off. He started to turn the volume back up, but then he heard it again. Something metallic sounding rattled in the yard. He could hear it as if it was right on top of him. He thought about it for a second. The trash did get picked up tomorrow and Hanna had taken the trash out earlier. Maybe it was a stray dog trying to dig through the trash for scraps.

His curiosity was sparked. Max climbed out of the recliner and went to the door to take a look.

He peered through the peephole in the door and flicked the switch for the porch light. The sudden harsh light illuminated the porch and beyond. Sure enough, one of the trashcans out by the road had been knocked over, but there was nothing around. No sign of an animal or anything. He knew that the weather said it was going to get bad, but there was no way the wind had blown it over. It hadn't gotten that bad out… yet. He thought of going outside to pick up the toppled can, but really didn't want to with the rain coming down like it was. His eyes craned left and right, checking the tree line through the peep hole. None of the trees seemed to be blowing out of control… again, that was to say *yet.*

"What'cha doing?"

Max jumped, goose-bumps sliding up his arms and across the back of his neck. When he turned around, Hanna waited with a glass of iced tea. A single slice of lime floated at the top of the ice, just how Max liked it.

"Thanks, honey," he said, shaking his head and taking the drink.

"Scared much?" She asked, giggling as she walked across the living room to take a seat back at her embroidery station.

"Something tipped one of the trashcans over," he insisted, trying to justify the startle.

Hanna just laughed.

He didn't bother trying to explain it. To give reason to the fright would only ensure her that he had been gotten good. And he didn't need that. She wouldn't let him live that one down for a long time. Either that or until he got her back with one good unexpected startle.

He smiled at the thought.

He then shrugged it off, giving her due credit for the scare and took a seat back in the recliner. He would go out and pick the trash up when the rain slowed some. He took a few sips of tea and found something to watch on TV. *Dexter's Laboratory*. So what if he was 30 years old. You were never too old for cartoons. And since Boomerang started showing it instead of Cartoon Network, he was starting to feel his age. Oh well… It was one of the episodes where DeeDee was messing around in his lab when she shouldn't. Come to think of it, that was just about every episode.

They sat there for a while, Max laughing at Dexter getting mad at his sister, and Hanna lost in the world of embroidery.

When the knock at the door broke the silent comfort, this time it was Hanna that jumped. Only it was less like a knock and more like a thump. Something heavy had just slammed against their front door. Both Max and Hanna stared at one another for a moment. Then it happened again. The violent *thud* made Max turn off the television and jump to his feet.

"What is it?" Hanna whimpered, setting her needlepoint stuff to the side.

"No idea, love." Max lifted a finger to suggest she hang tight for a second. He cautiously walked to the door and looked through the peephole. "It's Rose and her son, Paul, from across the street."

"Oh…" Hanna smiled, the tension instantly lifted. "She said she was going to bring some soup over later."

"Why does she always cook so damn much?" Max rolled his eyes. "That kid of hers ain't eating it, so why does she feel the need to make us eat it? He's a sack of sticks."

"She's just trying to be nice," Hanna said, very mater-of-fact. "And besides, cut her some slack. You know things have been tough on her since the auto accident. Now, invite them in already. They're probably soaking wet."

"Yeah…" Max agreed, turning the doorknob and opening the door. "Hey, Ro—

Rose lunged forward, forcing the door to slam hard into Max. He fell back, trying to catch himself, his footing off balance. He tumbled hard to the floor hitting his back against the wall.

Hanna screamed.

When Max looked up, puzzled by what was happening, his mouth dropped open in disbelief. Hanna was being attacked... attacked by Ms. Rose Stellie. Hanna fought against her attacker. Rose thrashed violently, hissing and grunting with rage. That was when Max noticed the blood. Rose was covered in it. Before he had the chance to stand to his feet and defend his wife, Paul stepped through the doorway and locked eyes with him. The teenager's hands were covered in blood. Red ran down from a gaping hole in his throat where his Adam 's apple should have been. The cavity was dark in the center and seeped puss and plasma, covering his shirt with blood.

Thunder boomed from outside.

"Oh, my God..." That was all Max was able to mutter before the Flea Market bag-boy charged at him with both hands out ready to kill.

Max lifted his legs and kicked as hard as he could, using the wall at his back as leverage. Paul staggered backward. The momentary distance forced Max to action. He stood to his feet trying to calm the teen. Paul didn't respond to his calming tone. Just before the kid charged him again, Max looked over the young man's shoulder across the living room. Hanna was still in trouble. Rose was on top of her, his wife pinned between the crazed neighbor and the recliner she had been sitting in before.

Paul hissed, spitting bloody saliva across the carpet, and leaped toward Max again.

This time, the auto-repair man was ready. He sidestepped just in time, grabbing the teen by the arm. Using Paul's momentum, Max shoved him as hard as he could right into the wall. Paul slammed into it hard. The bone shattering thump sent chills down Max's spine. When Paul turned around to face Max again, the wall where his face had hit was smeared with crimson. The bag-boy hissed again, his wide maw showing missing teeth. When Max sidestepped the next attack by Paul, he saw teeth actually imbedded into the wall out of the corner of his eye.

"What the fuck is happening?" Max screamed, shoving Paul headlong into the flat screen TV. Dexter's Laboratory was instantly obliterated when Paul's head went through the screen and into the wall on the other side. With his head still shoulder deep in the television, Paul fell limp right there, his knees hitting the carpet and his arms flaccid.

Max stood there for a moment taking it all in. This couldn't be really happening. He was sitting in the recliner having a crazy day-dream; the result of not wanting to take the vacation that work forced him to take. However, he wasn't snapping out of it. No, this was real. He heard the slurping grunts and gurgles. It forced him to look up. When he did, the sight before him made his chest drop into his feet. He felt woozy and lightheaded. Rose was leaning over Hanna. There was blood everywhere. Hanna wasn't moving. Her eyes were wide and vacant.

"What have you done?" Max breathed, his words choked out by disbelief.

Rose stopped what she was doing to Hanna and looked up at him. Max swallowed hard, frozen in fear. Rose was covered in blood. Hanna's blood. When she shifted her weight to look up at him, he caught a glimpse of what was happening. She had blood all over her hands. The meat dangling from her lips as she snarled at him fell to the carpet. It was Hanna's flesh. Rose was eating her!

Slowly, Rose stood up from Hanna's unmoving body and locked eyes with Max. Her eyes were mad with rage. Chunks of flesh fell from her hands as she raised them at him. The wet slap the meat made when it hit the carpet made Max's stomach churn.

"Rose…" Max pleaded, his voice brittle. "Why?"

Rose roared an animalistic grunt and charged at him.

She hit him head on and Max stumbled backward. Her teeth chomped violently over and over again. As they collided together, his neighbor's chomping teeth were like *clamping* vices that rang in Max's ears. Still back peddling, he held her head at bay with his hand held at her throat. His hand felt wet and warm against the gaping cavity where her throat should be. That was when he realized her neck was the same as Paul's. He stole a glance at Paul lying motionless on the floor, his head still in the TV.

Fear flooded Max's mind as he wrestled with his neighbor, who was just supposed to be bringing some soup over. What the hell was going on? He shoved her hard, providing distance between them. Not knowing what to do, he reached up on the wall and yanked down a framed photo he and Hanna had taken the last time they had gone to Disney World. It had been just before the big move to NC. In the photo, Goofy was kissing Hanna, and Max was acting shocked. It had turned out to be a cute photo. When the frame came down, it came down hard. He swung with everything he had. Glass shattered across Ms. Stellie's head. The frame came apart in his hands and Rose fell back from him, falling to the floor.

That was his chance.

He turned to head toward the kitchen, but not before taking one last look at Hanna. She was breathing. She was still alive.

A loud *thud* drew his attention to the front door. The front door was still wide open. The rain outside was getting so rough that the wind was forcing itself into the doorway. The carpet was becoming soaked with each droplet that entered, landing on the carpet. Old man Ryan C. Perish was shambling toward the door and had stumbled to his knees trying to get through the door. The old man was soaking wet. But something was wrong with him. He was dead. He had to be. His skin was pale and he was wearing nothing but his underwear. He was covered in blood from head to toe, the rain not doing much to wash it off his clammy body. But that wasn't what was wrong. It wasn't the hole in his throat like Rose and Paul. No, he didn't have a hole in his throat. He had a fucking hole the size of a damn basketball where his stomach should have been. His insides had spilled out. Chunks of meat and a link of intestine dangled down to his knees from the globular tumor of a hole. Unlike Rose and Paul, he didn't charge forward. He was still at the door, struggling to maintain balance while he entered the house.

"What the fuck!" Max screamed.

From his peripheral, he saw Rose starting to get up. He craned his neck and stole a glance at Hanna. He had to do something.

He turned and ran toward the kitchen.

I need something. Hanna needs me. He panted, racing into the kitchen while trying to make sense of it all. *The bedroom!*

Three Christmases ago, Hanna's father had given him a revolver. He wasn't much of a gun person. In fact, he hadn't even taken the time to get familiarized with the revolver. He'd never shot it before. Even still, it was in the bedroom, probably still sitting in the box it had been wrapped in, hidden in the back of the closet collecting dust. He rounded the corner, passing through the kitchen. Hanna had left the pitcher of tea out. She did that a lot and would later complain as if Max had been the one to leave it out.

In the bedroom, he closed the door and darted to the closet. Shoving clothing aside, he sifted through the boxes on the floor among the plethora of shoes Hanna owned but never wore.

"Come on… come on… I know you're in here."

It wasn't.

"Shit…" He panicked. "The bed!"

He turned, falling flat on the floor and digging under the bed. The box was there. When he pulled it out, tearing it open, he heard Rose hunting for him. It was as if she were some type of wild animal. He cradled the revolver and gritted his teeth, while trying to work the small box of bullets open. The box fell open, the bullets scattering across the carpet.

The loud crash at the bedroom door startled him.

"Fuck… fuck… fuck…" he gasped, falling to his knees and scooping bullets into his hand.

The door shook pugnaciously, Rose's pounding relentless. It was a surprise the door didn't come down with her giving it hell like that.

With his nerves shot, he struggled to force the bullets into the revolver. It was as if the bullets were too thick to go into the little holes. Finally, one slid into place… and then another, and another. With six bullets chambered, he stood to his feet and stuffed what bullets were left in his front pocket. He gritted his teeth, hoping like hell that the gun would fire. It hadn't been oiled or maintained; not once.

He aimed the gun at the shaking door. Grunts and hissing bellowed out from the other side.

Max thought of Hanna lying there dying in the living room. "Why are you doing this, Rose?" He started to cry. "Have you gone mad?"

Of course she had. She busted down his damn door and starting eating his wife!

With his finger on the trigger, he tried to steady his hands but couldn't. Whether it was the fear or the fact he wasn't ever really comfortable with guns, it didn't matter. He needed to pull it together. The thought of Hanna surfaced again and something came over him. His hands quit shaking and his nerves became more focused. The sickness trying to overtake his stomach subsided and he knew what he needed to do.

Funny thing, when you think about it.

Although Hanna loved watching horror movies, Max never really could stomach them. Blood, guts and violence just weren't his cup of tea. Even if they came with a lemon to top it off. But when you are faced with real life, it goes to show that you can do just about anything when forced in a corner. The love of your life is in danger and needs medical attention and the only thing between you and getting her that help is a crazy bitch that can't cook to save her life. Then there was Ryan and Paul. He didn't even want to think about Ryan, the town drunk. Someone walking around with that big of a hole in them, just wasn't plausible. And Paul... what he had done to Paul. He could have killed him. If that's what it was going to come down to, then so be it. If death was what stood in between him and saving Hanna, well... he thought the—

The door blew open, Rose tearing it from its hinges.

Max screamed, simultaneously squeezing the trigger for the first time ever.

Rose plummeted toward him. The revolver jolted in his firm grip. Although he was ready for the recoil, it burned his palms. Smoke fluttered from the barrel and Max watched the bullet do its damage.

It tore the flesh from her shoulder like melted butter. The blood sprayed from the exit wound across the wall and Rose didn't even flinch. She just kept coming.

Max screamed again and felt bile start to rise in his throat. He squeezed the trigger again, and just when Rose was about to grab hold, the bullet caught her in the left eye. Her eye socket exploded, slashing miasma and blood across Max's face and chest. She fell limp to the floor at his feet. All the while, Max could hear the bullet rattling around in her skull, turning her brain into potted meat.

Rose fell to the floor at his feet.

Max tried to take a breath, but vomited instead. His gut tightened like a metal vice and the dinner Hanna had cooked earlier, along with the iced tea, flowed out like a river all over Rose's corpse.

The smell and the sight of her at his feet made his stomach churn even more. His knees started to buckle, but he forced his body to move. Hanna was in trouble. His mind was so set on helping her that he completely forgot about old man Perish.

Leaving the bedroom and rounding the hallway corner into the kitchen, he almost ran right into the old drunk's arms. The old man groaned, startling Max to attention. He sidestepped and lifted the barrel of the gun against his head. Just when the old man started to shift his weight to advance, Max pulled the trigger. The loud report of the gun reverberated off the tile floor. Max's ears rang as he watched the old man's brain explode out the back side of his head.

Max didn't even stop to look or think. There would be time for that later. Right now, Hanna needed him.

Within seconds, he was in the living room and at her side. Ignoring the wide open front door and the mess of bodies scattered across his home, he cradled her in his arms.

"It's going to be okay, honey." He wiped blood from her face. "I'm going to get help."

She was cold and she wasn't breathing anymore.

Her eyes were lifeless and staring at nothing.

Emotion overwhelmed him like a flood as he pulled her into himself and cried.

Hanna was dead, her throat and face gushing blood where Rose had taken out chunks with her teeth.

He sat there covered in muck and blood, holding her, crying and confused.

*****

When Paul's stomach started to make noise, Max was too lost in everything to notice. Hanna needed him and he had failed.

The sound was wet like squishing gelatin between your fingers.

Paul Stellie's stomach split open, spilling out more than a dozen writhing things from the sea.

The storm was just beginning.

THREE

The Atlantic coast was wet.

Tropical Storm Faye was at a standstill and growing larger every hour. With the edge of the storm just off the coast, the mainland of North Carolina's boarder, along with the entire island of Topsail Beach were getting hit hard with waves of torrential rain. The heavy winds neared record highs for this early in the hurricane season and things were only going to go downhill from there.

*****

Max was still crying, holding his unmoving wife in his arms on the living room floor when he finally snapped out of panic mode. He needed to call for help. He sniffled, wiping the tears from his face, as he took one more look down at his wife's mangled face. Rose had done a number on her.

"I love you, baby. I'm sorry… I just—"

Max felt something slimy and wet crawl across his arm.

Startled, he jumped, looking down at the wiggling thing inching its way up. Slime trailed from Paul, whose head was still in the television, all the way across the carpet to Max.

He jumped to his feet and grabbed at the strange bug pulling its way up his arm. It bit him on the hand and he flung it to the floor.

"What the fuck?" He quivered, stomping the bug under his work-boot. "What the hell was that?"

When he lifted his foot to take a look, whatever it had been wasn't recognizable anymore. It was just a black smear of thick goo on the carpet. A sour smell rose and permeated the air. It smelled like a mixture of dead fish and dog shit. That was when Max heard the gurgling *drip-drip-drip* coming from Paul's body. There were more of those things he had just stepped on—all heading right at him. They squirmed across the carpet like oversized slugs. The trail of slime that followed in their wake was clearly the source of that awful stench. But they didn't look exactly like slugs. They looked more like tiny little squids. They were gray and covered in slime and bits of red. The red trailed behind along with the goo. When Max's eyes followed it, he found himself looking at the bagboy's stomach. It was wide open like old man Perish's had been.

Max's heart began to race. With more than a dozen of those little wiggling things headed toward him on the floor, he lifted his boot stomping each one that got too close. With each squishing *splat*, a faint dog-like yelp echoed out from under his heel.

Once they were all dealt with, whatever the hell they were, he took a deep breath. He needed to pull himself together. Needed to wrap his mind around what the hell was happening. Needed to call someone.

"Oh, my Lord!" Someone called out.

Max looked up. George Braidy stood in the doorway, the rain pouring down behind him. He was drenched.

George Braidy was a short, yet big, old man and had lived in the house next door for what he claimed to be more than 55 years. How that was possible, Max and Hanna never questioned, because the house next door wasn't more than 10 years old. Max knew this from when they were looking at houses online before the big move from up north. Despite that, George had turned out to be a great next door neighbor. He loved to fish and drink. Shortly after meeting the 67 year old man, Max had decided fishing and drinking were all there really was to do around Topsail. He and George had spent many weekends in the early morning out on the water in George's boat, casting nets and kicking back the cold ones. The old man loved his beer, but would always have a flask ready. All the old guys on the island seemed to have those damn things. Silly thing was, Max saw himself starting to truly turn into a local after hanging out with George. Just the other day, he caught himself eyeing flasks on the display rack at the grocery store. He talked himself out of getting one and instead just laughed at how much George reminded him of a plump Santa. If the old man ever took the time to grow out his beard, he probably could have pulled off the Santa thing. Max had mentioned it the last time they went out fishing. George didn't seem to be amused, so Max dropped it. They mostly talked about the same things; fishing, drinking, football, and music. George loved to talk music. He was a big fan of Hank Williams and Johnny Cash. Max never really listened to any of that, unless he was with George. He didn't mind. It just wasn't his cup of tea. He needed limes in his music. But he never mentioned that to George. The big old man seemed like the kind of guy that would think him queer for listening to stuff like Memphis May Fire, Underoath, and Truly, Truly. Music was one thing, but if the old man ever found out about him and his need to watch cartoons… that would have been the one to end things for sure. The old man was an all-American and didn't really understand stuff like metal and watching cartoons at the age of 30.

"What the hell happened?"

"I… I… I don't know," Max whimpered, looking down at the gun in his right hand. "Hanna… I think she's…"

"Oh, my God." George gasped, stepping into the living room, grabbing Max by the arm, and pulling him out onto the porch. "Here, let me see that."

George took the revolver from Max and told him to sit down. He complied, taking a seat in one of the rocking chairs he and Hanna had bought shortly after moving into the house. A tear rolled down his cheek at the thought of buying them together. Max couldn't hold it in any longer. If he started crying again, he wasn't sure he would ever be able to stop. He swallowed hard to keep the tears at bay. A dense fog rolled into his mind, numbing it. He looked up at George, who was standing next to him on his cell phone, the panicked expression across his face, letting Max know that all of this was real. Even though he could see the big man's mouth moving with the phone to his ear, he couldn't hear him. He couldn't hear anything. After all that had just happened, Max's body was shutting down. His arms felt limp as if they weren't even attached. His body felt like one big fat lifeless sack. His mind was sludge. He couldn't process any of it. The lines were beginning to blur. There just was no way Hanna was really dead.

"Police and paramedics are on the way," George said, slapping the phone shut and stuffing it into his jean pocket. "If I had to guess it's gonna be quite some time before they get here. With the weather like it is, things are going to be pretty backed up in Surf City." George paused, digging some tobacco dip from his back pocket, pinching off a bit of chew. He stuffed it deep at the back of his cheek, puffing it out. Putting the can away, he said, "Now, Max. What the hell happened?"

Max didn't say anything. He couldn't even look up at the old man. His body worked against him, and he just sat dazed in the rocking chair.

"Max... I'm going to go in and take a look, okay?" George said, calmly. "The medics are going to be running slow getting here. I want to make sure no one in there needs any immediate help. Okay?" George paused for a second and then continued. "Okay then... I'll be back in just a second."

When George turned to walk back into the house, Max finally found strength over his body again.

Grabbing the plump old man by the arm, he said, "No, don't go in there."

"What's wrong?" George spit tobacco juice out past the porch into the pouring rain.

The wind increased dramatically. The rain beat against them both on the porch like sharp little needles. They hadn't even been out on the porch more than a few minutes and Max was already just as soaked at the old man. His skin was cold, the needle-like drops of rain reminding him of Hanna and her needlepoint with each bead that beat against his damp skin.

"I don't know. Just don't go in there, man."

"I have to go see. Someone might need help in there, Max."

"The squid…" Max breathed. "They came out of Paul's belly. They tried to get to me. Get inside of me."

"What the hell are you talkin' about, boy?"

"One of them bit me on the hand." Max raised his hand. There were puncture marks and blood between his thumb and forefinger.

"Who… Paul? The bag-boy kid bit you? Who did this?"

"No... The little squids. One of them bit me."

"You're not makin' much sense, Max. I need to go see if—"

"I killed Rose Stellie," Max said, cutting George short.

"The nice lady from across the street that always cooks for all of us?" George gasped.

"And Ryan Perish. He's in the kitchen. I shot him in the head. Rose was the one that did that to Hanna. I'm telling you… don't go in there. There's something wrong. Ryan shouldn't have even been alive. And the squid, they squirmed out of Rose's son's stomach. I'm telling you the truth. I know it sounds crazy."

"But, Max…" George said, trying to pull away.

"I know how it sounds. Believe me," Max insisted, wiping rainwater from his face. "Listen to my voice. I haven't lost it. I'm sane. We've been neighbors for a long time, George. Please… don't go in there."

"Okay… Okay, Max. I won't," George said, spitting tobacco juice out into the yard again. "Let's at least get out of the rain until the police and paramedics get here. I'll close the door and we can wait over at my house for them to arrive…okay? I can call the station back in Surf City and let them know where we'll be. In the meantime, you can tell me what happened over a warm cup of coffee and something dry to wear."

Max nodded, and followed George next door when the rain lightened up a bit.

George Braidy's house was quaint.

Having never married, his home was the cliché of all bachelor pads. Well, not really. He was pretty old after all. And with old age came the conservative perspectives of his generation. His living room was the only room in the house Max had ever been in. For all he knew, it was the only room George lived in. The fireplace was lined with stone all the way up the wall. On either side of the fireplace on the same wall were what George claimed to be his pride and joy. On the left side there was a stuffed duck, taxidermy to perfection. It was positioned in flight, hung to the wall by a large petrified slice of wood. At the bottom of the wood was a small gold-colored engraving with the number 43 on it. The number of birds brought down that day by the big man himself. He was proud of it and loved telling the story. Max knew, because he had heard the story over a dozen times while over having drinks and playing cards after a long day at the auto shop. On the other side of the fireplace was the head of a deer. It was a lot smaller than some of the ones Max had seen before. And the horns really weren't that impressive. It was only an eight point buck. Regardless, just like that duck, George was proud of it. The story that went with that trophy was kind of silly, and Max actually enjoyed hearing it over and over again. Apparently, the old man hadn't even been out more than ten minutes when the deer strolled up on him. By what he says in the story, he was still climbing into his tree stand when he dropped his gun. It went off when it hit the ground and the deer miraculously took the bullet in the neck of all places. The only deer the old man ever took down, too.

His furniture was old and musty. The television was so small and outdated Max was surprised the old man even knew what a TV was.

It had been a few minutes.

Max sat on the dusty old couch, a cup of coffee warming his hands. He was sopping wet and practically comatose. He had yet to even take a sip from the mug of coffee. His mind was numb to everything. Hanna just couldn't be dead. Just no way.

"Here—take this," George said, handing him a towel. "You're soaked."

Max nodded, setting the cup down on the coffee table and took the towel. While he dried off, George looked at him long and hard. When he finally spoke, his tone was soft and concerned.

"I talked to the police. Told 'em we'd be here. Gonna be a bit since the storm's brewin'." George shifted the chew in his mouth from one cheek to the other, and then spit the dark juice into a water bottle. "Look, Max. I'm sorry about Hanna. I really am. I can't even imagine what you're going through. Your head has to be going a million miles in every other direction. I get it. I really do. But you need to talk. We need to get your story straight. The cops are gonna want to know what happened. What the hell *did* happened in there? And don't tell me this mess about squids coming out of people. I know Hanna liked watching those horror flicks. Your mind is just confused. With everything happening so fast, your mind's just jumbled. Messed up... I just think you—"

"I know what I saw..." Max breathed, his words almost inaudible.

"But, Max... little squids trying to get inside of you?"

"Yes, George. They came out of that boy… Paul. They were mad. Him and his mom. And Ryan. You didn't see Ryan." Max raised his voice, "The man's fucking stomach was hanging out like on The Walking Dead!"

"What… like that show on TNT?"

"Yeah… Her face, George. Rose was eating her face!"

"Look… calm down, okay? We'll get this all straightened out when the police get here." George took a seat across from Max. Dust floated up from the chair when he sat down. He propped up his boots on the coffee table, spit more tobacco juice into his water bottle and said, "But right now, maybe we don't need to rehash this. You've been through enough already as it is. Let's just sit tight and wait for them to get here. Is there anything else I can get you? A dry shirt…"

"I don't think it would fit me," Max said, forcing a smile to the surface.

They both laughed at the prospect of Max, who was more than half the size of the old man fitting into one of his shirts. But the laughter faded fast, Max's expression returning to solemn dread and despair.

"No… really," George cleared his throat. "Can I get you anything, buddy?"

Max locked eyes with the old man, trying like hell to keep a straight face.

That was when the floods came. Max couldn't hold it in any longer. He sat there, the towel in his hand, the coffee on the table in front of him, crying. The sobs flowed and no matter how much he tried to stop, tried to be a real man in front of George, he just couldn't.

George didn't say anything.

They just sat for a long time while Max let it all out, one vehement tear at a time.

When the knock at the door finally came, Max jumped.

The expression plastered across his face screamed, *Don't open that door.*

"It's just the police," George assured, climbing out of his chair. "I can see the lights flashing outside."

George answered the door, Max still glued to the couch. The muffled conversation slid across the living room like the dust covering the old man's furniture.

"Yes, officer. He's in here." George paused, and said, "Yes, sir. Case of self-defense… Yes, sir. Come on in."

The policeman entered the room and took a seat across from Max. Taking off his hat, water dripped to the floor as he set it on the coffee table. He was covered in rain water. It must have really been coming down out there. And to remind Max of that fact, a loud boom of thunder echoed out so loudly, the deer head on the wall shook in place, almost ready to fall off the wall.

The police officer was a young man. Everybody called him J.J. He was a good guy. Treated everybody fairly and tried to see all sides of it. Most people said he wasn't very experienced, but he had been a cop for as long as Max and Hanna had lived in the area.

"Max," the officer started. "I'm sorry to hear about Hanna. George here told me that Rose and her son entered your home and attacked the both of you. As much as I can't much fathom that to be true… is it?"

Max nodded and looked to George, who was giving him a stern glare. The large man's eyes said, *'Don't you dare tell him all the nonsense you told me about the squid.'*

Max took a deep breath, nodded at George and let out with it. "Yeah, J.J., that's what happened."

"That just doesn't make sense." J.J. shrugged.

"Do you want anything to drink?" George asked, tapping J.J. on the shoulder.

"No, I'm good," J.J. said, looking up at him. "We need to get going anyway. I haven't been in the house, but the paramedics have and they said it's a mess. Never seen anything like it."

"What do we do?"

"You don't have to do anything, George," Officer J.J. insisted. "But Max, unfortunately… you need to come with me. We need to go to the station and file a report. You can stay with us until this all gets straightened out."

"What?" George barked. "You can't be serious about putting him in jail. Not after all he's been through. He ain't no murderer, J.J.!"

"I know that, Mr. Braidy." J.J. stood to his feet and put his hat back on. "If I thought he was a killer, do you think I would be standing here right now? No, I would've cuffed him and thrown him in the back of the patrol car already… no offense." J.J. looked at Max.

"None taken." Max sniffled, wiping his swollen eyes.

J.J. nodded. "I know good people and bad people when I see 'em, okay?" The officer reached out, shaking George's hand and smiled. "Topsail only has a few bad eggs, and Max Willgood ain't one of those. Hell, the man's given me a discount on my junker of a truck more times than I can count. I'm surprised the damn thing still works. He knows autos."

"You ain't the only one he's helped out." George smiled, letting go of the officer's hand.

"But that doesn't change protocol. I'm sorry, Max, but I need to cuff you and put you in the back of the car… at least until we get to the station and square this all away, okay?"

J.J. made his move toward Max and George stepped forward as if he were going to do something about it. The large man's fist clenched tight.

"It's alright, George. I understand." Max sniffled again, wiping his nose across his forearm and stood to his feet. "Let's just go…"

"Well, I'm goin' with you," George demanded.

Max looked to the floor while J.J. applied the cuffs. "Thanks, George. I don't know if I could do this alone. I can't believe it, man. She really is gone. Isn't she?"

George didn't say anything.

The handcuffs clipping filled the silence instead.

Stepping around the couch, Max looked down at the steaming cup of coffee on the table. It was still just as full as when George had given it to him. They reached the door and J.J. opened it. With his hands bound behind his back, he stepped out onto the front lawn with the officer in the lead and George coming up behind him. The wind was kicking hard and the rain even harder. The tree limbs pointed toward the east along with the clothing on his back; the wind forcing them on. Had the wind picked up any more, Max wouldn't have been surprised if his clothing just up and blew right off his body. As they walked up to the sidewalk leading back toward the Willgood residence, a cascade of lights flashed in the sky. The darkness was illuminated with a flash of harsh reds, blues, and white. There were two patrol cars and the ambulance, all of which had their lights flashing.

"You gonna drive your own car, Mr. Braidy, or do you want to ride back to the station with us?"

"Riding with you would be just fine, so long as you can give us a ride back."

"I'm sure we can arrange that." J.J. grinned, opening the back passenger door to the cruiser. He helped Max climb in and he shut the door. "Door's unlocked if you want to go ahead and take a seat, George. I'm gonna step inside and let the other officer know that we have Max in custody and are heading back into town."

George nodded and climbed into the front passenger seat of the police car. The rain beat down on the door like tiny little pellets. In any other circumstance, the droning sound would have been soothing. It was anything but. Max just sat there, listening to the rain, with the water dripping into the seat from his soggy body. The short trip from George's house to the car was enough to make him ten pounds heavier with water. His wet clothes weighed down on him and when he took a deep breath and let it out, the window began to fog up.

"It's gonna be okay, Max," George whispered, while they watched J.J. trudge across the yard into Max's house.

The flashing lights illuminated the entire yard, even the bloodstains leading into his living room on the carpet that the rain had yet to wash away.

Max whimpered, staring at the house… at the home that he and his wife had spent the last some odd years building. Through the doorway, he could barely make out one of her yarn art pieces hanging on the wall.

Just when the tears started to flow anew, someone screamed.

It came from inside the house.

FOUR

J.J.'s police uniform was illuminated by the cacophony of flashing lights as he darted out the front door and stumbled to the grass in Max's yard. With both hands out to catch his fall, his knees and palms collided with the soggy landscape. Water splashed up around him, his expression filled with terror.

When he turned toward the house, staggering backward on the grass, his police hat fell off.

George gasped, as both he and Max watched from their vantage point inside the patrol car.

One of the paramedics darted out of the house. She fell to her knees on the porch, the porch light revealing every gory detail. She was covered in gray little spots about the size of soda cans. But the spots were moving. They were all over her arms, chest, and face. The woman screamed, grabbing at her throat with both hands.

That was when it happened.

Blood jutted from her throat like a child squirting a water gun. The blood sprayed out nearly to where J.J. was sitting in the grass. Max thought of the hole he had seen in both Rose's and her son's throat. That's what it had to be. One of those things was getting into the paramedic. As if to justify his thought process, the woman's hands fell from her throat to her sides, the wiggling tentacles forcing their way down into her body.

Just as J.J. pulled the 9mm from his hip and aimed it toward the porch, the paramedic fell limp.

"What the fuck was that?" George gasped, his eyes wide.

"Exactly what I told you!" Max demanded. "Those things that came out of Paul Stellie's belly. We got to get out of here, man."

"But the—" George's sentence was cut short, his jaw dropping open by what happened next.

The other paramedic, a male wearing a yellow rain coat, came running out of the house. Only, his rain coat was covered in blood. He ran right past the woman lying motionless on the porch. Just when anyone would have expected to see him run past J.J. and toward the ambulance, he didn't. He charged right at J.J. who seemed to be just as perplexed as Max and George. Just before the paramedic fell on the police officer, Max saw a hole in the throat of the paramedic wearing the raincoat. Those things had gotten inside of him, too.

He fell on J.J., thrashing and snapping his teeth, ready to taste the first meaty morsel that dared get within biting distance. J.J. fell to his back in the grass using his free hand to wrestle with the attacker. The 9mm went off twice, the loud report sounding more like thunder than an actual gunshot.

"Shit, George..." Max spat. "Get out there and help'em!"

"I ain't goin' out there! You crazy?"

"Well, I sure as hell can't do it!" Max shouted, lifting his shoulders to remind the large old man that he was still cuffed. "Now, go!"

"Mother fucker..." The old man breathed. He shook his head, locked eyes with Max once, and then stepped out into the pouring rain.

There was nothing Max could do, and at the moment, his mind was as far away from Hanna as it could get. He was too focused on the chaos unfolding in his front yard. He just watched on from inside the cruiser, both hands behind his back. His heart raced as he watched George trudge over to J.J. like a staggering sack filled with potatoes. He reached out, grabbing hold of J.J.'s attacker and lifted him off of the officer. That was when the pistol went off again. The paramedic in the yellow rain coat fell limp right then and there. It was hard for Max to see, but with the way the man's head had jolted when the gun went off, it was a clear shot to the skull. The rain was coming down hard. With his back to the house, George leaned over to help J.J. to his feet.

Then the woman that had fallen to her knees on the porch started to get back up.

Max screamed, "Look out!"

It was no use. They couldn't hear him.

Just before the woman started to charge forward, toward J.J. and George, the other officer that J.J. had gone in to talk to came running out. He sprinted right past the woman, colliding with the heavyset fisherman. George fell to his knees and the police officer attacking him reared back with a ravenous snarl. The officer bit down hard on the back of George's neck. Max watched him scream in agony, but didn't hear a single sound from inside the patrol car.

J.J. lifted his pistol, trying to take aim, but the struggle was too sporadic. He couldn't clear a shot without the risk of shooting George. Max wasn't sure if that was what was happening, but that was what it looked like.

The woman on the porch charged forward with her arms raised.

Max screamed again, trying to warn them. As if it had actually worked this time, J.J. shifted his aim. The gun shook in his hand three times. With each convulsing motion, the woman jolted, taking a bullet in the chest. Blood spewed from each entry wound. Still practically in full sprint, she hit the ground running.

George still screamed and struggled with the policeman on his back.

J.J. didn't even hesitate. He turned away from the woman on the ground, and as if he had done it a thousand times in training, he reached up, grabbing the other cop by the shirt collar and shoved the barrel of his pistol in the man's temple. Max felt the tension gripping at his chest. He didn't even realize he had been holding his breath. When J.J. pulled the trigger, the meaty chunks of pulp that blew out the other side glistened a harsh flash of blues, reds, and white before slopping down in the wet grass, the lights from the patrol cars and ambulance still covering the yard.

The police officer fell off George and then there was stillness.

J.J. stood there for a moment longer, the 9mm still raised as if he were still holding the gun into the dead man's temple. George sat in the grass, paralyzed, or in shock. Max couldn't tell. He looked bad. He was holding the back of his neck. Max couldn't tell if it was just the rain or if it was blood, but whatever was all over the back of George's shirt, it was soaked in deep.

The wind continued to blow heavily around them.

Max watched as J.J. helped George to his feet. It seemed as if an eternity passed while they both stood assessing the situation and talking to one another. All the while, George kept one hand held at the back of his neck and he kept wincing. It didn't look good.

Max finally took a deep breath, realizing that he had been holding it the entire time.

Both of his friends in the yard nodded at one another. George turned, wading through the wet grass and falling rain back toward the patrol car. J.J., on the other hand, turned and made his way back into the house, pistol at the ready.

When George entered the patrol car, Max felt the cold rush of gusting winds.

"Oh, Jesus," Max groaned, looking at the back of George's neck.

"I'll… I'll be okay," George said in mid-swallow.

"I don't know, man. That guy got you good."

"Guy?" George laughed, wincing at the same time. "Don't you mean, '*that thing*'? You were serious, weren't you? What you said about Rose and the kid…"

Max paused before he spoke. "Yeah…" His tone sounded regretful.

"Fuckin' hell," George continued, dabbing at the back of his neck and head. "That ain't no shit, Max. That woman was covered in those things. And that cop's throat. If I ever say you were talking shit ever again in my life, it'll be the end of me. I'm sorry I ever dou—"

"We can talk 'told you so' later, old man," Max said. "Where the hell did J.J. go? He isn't going to find anything in there. We need to leave. And now. Hell, you need a doctor, George."

"I don't know. Said he was just going to take a look. Said he *had* to."

"Fuck that!"

"Yeah, that ain't no shit," George agreed, pulling his hand away from his wound and seeing a mixture of blood and rainwater dripping from his fingers. "My freakin' neck is burnin'."

"Let me take a look."

George leaned forward in an effort to give Max a better view of the wound.

"I can't see much. Is there a light up there that you can turn on?"

George looked up and pressed the button over his head, turning on the interior light.

"Let me see…" Max said, leaning up in his seat to get a better look. "Looks like it hurts, man, but I think you'll live."

"But the bite?"

"What about it?" Max raised a brow.

"Ain't it gonna get infected or somethin'?"

"Not as long as we can get you to the doctor to clean it up soon. What's taking J.J. so long?" He asked, craning his neck to look toward the house. "We don't have time for this. We need to go."

"No, I mean, like in that television show of yours."

"What, *The Walking Dead* on TNT?"

"Yeah, didn't those people turn when they got bit?"

"Yeah, but I don't think this is like that."

"How do you know?" George's voice was filled with panic.

"Look, man, I don't… We just need to get you to a doctor."

They both sat there in silence for a few minutes watching the house. The front door was still wide open, the living room light still on. The dead police officer and the two paramedics still laid motionless on the lawn, the emergency flashers and porch light casting every bit of it for them to see. Like staring at the sun for too long, it started to burn into the back of Max's retina. Just when he couldn't take looking at it anymore, one of the bodies moved.

The female paramedic's body twitched and convulsed on the ground.

"Did you see that?"

"See what?" George asked, squinting his eyes.

It was hard to see past the rain running down the windows.

"That lady. She moved!"

"That's not possible, Max. I watched ole J.J. shoot that woman three times at nearly point blank range."

"Oh, yeah?" Max scoffed. "Just like squid looking motherfuckers trying to dig into your throat isn't real?"

They both took a closer look.

The woman moved again and this time, they both saw it and watched in absolute horror. Her midsection jerked hard to one side and her paramedic's uniform blew out in the middle. The woman's stomach exploded. Small gray things about the size of a soda can, just like Max had described it, spilled out of her belly. There were tons of them. They all scattered off in every direction, disappearing in the rain. Max was about to say '*See, I told you so*'. But he didn't have the chance. What happened next was so startling that it choked the words right out of his mouth like a thief in the night.

The woman stood to her feet. Her intestines and chunks of muck sagged from the open cavity that used to be her belly.

George made a sound as if he were about to vomit but held it back.

The woman staggered forward. She wasn't running like she had been before. No, she shuffled toward the patrol car, one uncoordinated step at a time. She was like a zombie. Like the ones in Max's TV show. Both men gasped in unison, watching her close the distance.

"I think I'm gonna throw up." George swallowed hard.

Then the two other bodies lying in the grass started to convulse at the same time.

"Oh, my God. It's happening to them, too."

Sure enough, both of the bodies jittered and shook momentarily just before their bellies ruptured, spilling out more than a dozen of those squirming critters.

"Those are gonna get up, too?" George asked, as if Max knew what the hell was going on just because Hanna liked to watch silly horror shows.

Oh... Hanna... Max's lip quivered.

Neither of those bodies got up. They just laid there motionless. Dead.

"Why ain't they gettin' up, Max?"

Max just ignored him, thinking of Hanna, but his thoughts of her were instantly pushed away. The dead woman staggering toward them was only a few feet from the car now. Rain drenched her from head to toe, the wind nearly knocking her off balance. Shifting her weight, she managed to resist the sudden gust of winds. She fell onto the car as if it were something to eat. She pounded on the hood and windows. Her midsection smeared across the windows right in front of Max and George. The blood and meaty chunks pressed against the glass. It smeared like chunky peanut butter and jelly. Only it wasn't brown and purple. It was dark red and flesh colored. A piece of recognizable meat from her insides surfaced, pressing against the glass. That, added to the grunting and groaning she was already doing while she pounded on the hood was just too much.

George vomited.

The steaming pile of steak and potatoes he had eaten for dinner slid across his chest and down his robust belly. The smell was sour and rank, making Max gag. He wanted more than anything to cover his mouth. He could taste it. But he was out of luck. His hands cuffed behind his back forced him to endure the taste and smell of recycled dinner.

Thunder boomed, followed by a flash of harsh bright light in the sky.

Both men jumped in their seats.

Just when George was about to apologize for throwing up, another report echoed out. Only it wasn't thunder. It was a gun shot. The woman fighting to get into the cruiser fell limp, sliding across the window. The gore and guts that smeared across the glass sticking to the window made George gag again.

When Max looked up, J.J. stood in place of the woman that had been trying to get in. Max felt relief flood over his being as he watched the young police officer round the front of the cruiser and climb into the driver's seat.

"Oh, thank God!"

J.J. didn't reply, yet. He reached down, taking the police radio in his hand. "Tina… come in! This is unit 3." The only sound that came back was a deafening squeal. "Tina… Come in." He looked out the window toward the house then slammed the radio into the floorboard at George's feet. "Fuck! I don't think God's awake tonight, boys!" J.J. slammed the car door shut and cranked the engine.

"That ain't no shit!" George agreed, wiping the puke from his lips.

"What the fuck's going on, J.J.?" Max shook his head

"Your guess is as good as mine." J.J. nodded, locking eyes with Max through the rearview mirror. "But one thing's for damn sure. I aim to find out. And that's where we're headed right now!"

"The only place we need to be headed is to the doctor. George's neck is wide open."

"Well…" J.J. said, glanced over at George, then jammed the cruiser into drive and peeled out in Max's yard. The car straightened out and started down the road. "Where we're going, we can get that taken care of. Looks like the bleeding's stopped anyway."

"We headed to the station?" George asked, touching his hand to the back of his neck, and then looking to see that it had actually stopped bleeding.

"No… We're going to Tatter's house."

"That dude's nuts. What the hell we doing going to his house? We need to go to the hospital or the station!"

J.J. didn't reply. He just drove.

Tension, stress, fear, and sorrow filled the silence.

The only sound they heard over the engine on the way to Tatter's was the rain beating down against the hood of the patrol car.

FIVE

Tatter Drake'o lived on the farthest end of the island clear across town on the opposite side of the Surf City Bridge.

He was an ornery old man, much like all the old men who lived in Topsail. Unlike George Braidy, he was married and had four kids. All his kids were grown now and had moved on to bigger and better things. His oldest was some big time journalist in New York and the others had moved to different parts of the country, doing whatever it was they were doing. He kept up with them from time to time online and over the phone. He never really was one for technology. His kids had set him up with a computer and high-speed internet. That was when things got weird.

When his wife passed away, like a lot of the older folks seemed to be doing these days, he fell off the deep end. Tatter found companionship in open cans of beer, which wasn't really that strange for Topsail. But the stuff he looked up on the computer sure as hell got stranger and stranger. Some of the stuff he would share at the bar was just bizarre. The conspiracies, the odd creatures of cryptozoology, and other strange phenomena that only he seemed to understand. His audience just let it go in one ear and out the other. They understood loneliness had him weirded out.

Like George, he was an avid fisherman. But he didn't fish for food. He fished for sport, always throwing back his catch. On the few occasions he would snag something worth its weight in story-telling, Tatter would get one of his friends to take a picture of him holding it before throwing it back.

The four men were in the kitchen.

George had a seat at the bar. Max leaned against the sink. J.J. stood by George, holding a wet rag and pair of scissors. Tatter hovered over George, bandaging his wound.

Standing behind George made Tatter look like nothing more than a toothpick. He was the exact opposite of George in size being tall and thin. Standing nearly 6'5", he probably didn't weigh a measly 150 lbs. Max was pretty sure he had only seen Tatter wear one outfit and he was wearing that same get-up now. He dressed in a slender pair of overalls and a plain white t-shirt. The shirt had permanent yellow stains under the arms. His thick bottle-cap glasses were round and made his eyes bulge on his narrow face. Before retirement, he was a welder and had the scars to prove it. His forearms were covered in long burn marks from years of the profession. Now, in his older age, the scars looked more like sunspots. He had one tattoo on his shoulder of a black bobcat. The animal's back feet and tail just barely peeked out from under his shirt sleeve. Much like the overalls he wore, the tattoo was faded.

"I don't know why you boys felt the need to come knocking on my door. I ain't no doctor, J.J." Tatter said, applying pressure to the wound. His voice was deep and robust, his Adam's apple bobbing up and down on that narrow neck.

George winced.

"I know, but—"

"But nothin', J.J." Tatter cut him short. He motioned for the cop to cut a few slices of tape to use to hold the bandage in place on the back of George's neck. "I didn't expect this out'a you."

"What's that supposed to mean?" J.J. cut three strips of tape, handing them to Tatter.

"Lack of experience as a cop is one thing, but coming in here like this… scaring the kids half to death and thinking I'm a doctor. Come on, boy. Where's your head?

And the silly stories. What the hell? Are you making fun of me and my theories?"

"The stories are true," Max breathed, shifting his body against the sink.

From his vantage point from the kitchen he could see into the living room. Tatter's next door neighbor was a single mother who worked nights at the all night diner in Surf City. At least three nights a week he agreed to baby sit her kids while she was at work. From what Max could tell, babysitting them wasn't much work. They were glued to the television playing some first person shooter video game. Peggy and Blake were brother and sister from two different fathers. Peggy was one year older than Blake. Max hadn't personally met them, but had seen them a few times before at the store. He wasn't great at guessing ages, but they couldn't have been more than ten years old. The sound of violence from the TV and laughter from the children echoed into the kitchen.

"Ain't no shit, Tatter," George agreed. "It's for real."

Tatter locked eyes with J.J. and rolled his eyes.

"Believe us, old man," J.J. demanded. "That's why we came to you."

"Look, boy. I know that I…" Tatter lowered his voice, looking toward the living room. "I know I've been off my rocker ever since Tammy died. But that don't give you the right to think I know what the hell to do about any of this. You're the policeman… or did you forget that already? You need to go to the station. File your little reports or whatever the hell it is you do and leave me and the kids out of this."

"Yeah…" Max agreed, leaning forward against the sink. When he craned his neck to look back into the living room, his eyes caught a quick glimpse of a photo on the refrigerator. It was of Tatter holding the biggest fish he had ever seen. The grin on the old man's face was even bigger. "We shouldn't have come here, J.J. What about Hanna?"

The kitchen fell silent for a minute.

Tatter finished bandaging up George's neck and went to the fridge for a beer, not offering one to anyone else. Everyone had that same blank stare, their eyes wide and locked on J.J.

Max took a deep breath and sighed. The sound of the children's video game filled the silence.

"Okay… look." J.J. lifted his hands in defeat. He walked over to the fridge. Tater stepped aside, and J.J. pulled a beer out for himself. Popping the top and taking a sip, he looked at Tatter and said, "I came here because I know you know what these things are."

"What the hell makes you think that he knows anything?" Max asked.

"Me and Tatter hang out a lot, okay?" J.J. took a deep gulp from his bottle and continued, "A lot of the stuff—conspiracies and junk—he finds of the internet are totally stupid. I get that. And I think he does, too. But there is one he showed me a few months ago. There were squid-like creatures on a website that looked just like these. We came here because I want you to show us. As much as going to the station seemed like the right thing to do… *what good would it do, huh*?" J.J. raised his voice. "The storm is blowing really hard. It would take forever to get over there. Tatter's house was closer. And yes… we should'a taken George to a real doctor. But, what good would that have done either? Trying to explain to them, or my captain for that matter, the stuff we saw… they just wouldn't believe me. Those people were crazed!"

He chugged the rest of the beer and turned around pulling another from the fridge. He popped the top and took a sip.

"Hell…" J.J. looked down at his shaking hands and continued. "I fuckin' killed another officer, Tatter. And two paramedics. This shit, what we're telling you, is real. You just need to believe that. I shot that woman three times in the chest. And she died."

"Yeah?" Tatter nodded.

"Then explain to me," J.J. chugged half of the beer in one long swig. "How the hell did that bitch get back up? When I came out of that house, she was still… God, man. The stuff I saw in that house, Tatter. You got to believe us."

"Hmmm…" Tatter stood for a minute, staring at the floor and sipping on his beer.

Tension filled the kitchen, growing so thick Max felt it around his throat like a violent man's bear grip. He almost couldn't breathe, and had to force himself to relax.

"Well?" J.J. said, downing the last bit of his beer.

Tatter nodded, drinking the rest of what beer he had left as well. "Okay then… Everybody grab a beer. You boys look like you could use 'em. Especially you, Max. Follow me."

Tatter opened the fridge and grabbed another beer for himself, then walked into the living room with the kids. J.J. followed suit and did the same. George climbed down from the barstool and walked over to Max, who remained leaning against the sink.

He sighed and reached up, grabbing the young auto repairman by the shoulder. "Look, Max. I know what you're thinking… Where the hell is all this going? To be honest, I don't know either. But what we saw back at your house, it just weren't natural. I know what we need to do. We need to go to the station and get someone over to the house to do a real investigation. Let's just see where this goes, okay? I'm with you. I'm ready to go. Let's give J.J. the benefit of the doubt on this one and give them at least 10 minutes. If we don't get somewhere with all of this by then, I will jack the kid's cop car myself… and we can go then. I just don't think he would'a brought us here for nothing. What happened back there don't make no sense. And even though I don't want to admit it, J.J. is right. If anybody, and I mean anybody, knows what the hell to do… it's gonna be Tatter. The old man might be a bit batty, but he knows his shit."

Max nodded, sagging his head between his shoulders.

George leaned in and gave him a hug. "It's gonna be all right… I think."

"I'll be okay," Max said, leaning into the old man's shoulders. "I don't know if I can do this. I just want to go home and go to bed. Maybe tomorrow this will—"

"I wish, Max. I really do."

That was when George turned and walked away, leaving his neighbor alone in the kitchen.

Max stood for a few minutes by himself. He could still see the kids playing the game. He stared long and hard at that photo on the refrigerator of Tatter holding up a monster of a fish. The smile plastered across the skinny man's face made him look crazy. Maybe they were all crazy. Just a bunch of loons living in a ward somewhere going along with this sick terrifying story. If that were the case, at least then Hanna wouldn't have been killed, because then she wouldn't have been real to begin with. What was he going to tell her parents? What was he going to tell himself tomorrow when he woke up and realized she wasn't going to be there anymore? No more waking up next to her smiling face in bed. No more embroidery. No more scary movies with her curled up beside him on the couch. No more Hanna. Max felt his stomach sink deep into his knees. He wasn't sure he wanted to find out the truth. Find out what those things were or where they came from. He just wanted them gone. Wanted to go back to that moment when he answered the front door. Knowing what he knew now, he would have told Rose to go fuck herself and that her cooking was shit. Would have never answered that door in the first—

"Hello… who are you?"

When Max looked up, he expected to see an angel. The girl's voice was so soft and innocent. It was Peggy. Her hair was straight and shiny, down to her shoulders. She was a tiny little thing. The shirt she wore was, of all things, Miss Piggy from the Muppets. He smiled at her and somehow felt the emotions subside.

"Hi… I'm one of Tatter's friends. My name is Max. You must be Peggy." He reached up, scratching his thick, dark mustache. "Am I right?"

"Yep…" She giggled.

"So, what game are you guys playing in there?"

"Time Crisis 5," she said, very matter-of-fact. "Blake is cheating."

"Well that's no fun."

"I don't want to play that game anymore," she said, running her fingers through her hair.

"Well, then. What game do you want to play?"

"I don't want to play games anymore. I want to watch Shrek."

"I remember that one. Do we have it?"

"Yeah… Mommy lets us bring lots of movies over when we spend the night with Mr. Tatter." She giggled.

"What's so funny?" Max asked, walking over to the refrigerator and getting a beer. Somehow the sorrows just washed away from him like a thousand pounds being lifted off of his chest. The life and innocence of this little girl flowed over him like a renewing spirit.

"Tatter…" she grinned wide, saying the word. "That's a funny name. My mommy says it's not his real name either."

Max laughed out loud. It felt invigorating. "I agree. It is a silly name. But don't tell him that. It might hurt his feelings."

"Okay…"

"So, did you come in here to get something?"

"No," she said. "I died on the game and Blake is still playing it."

"Well, let's go see about getting the game turned off and putting in that movie."

"Yay!" Peggy lit up like a Christmas tree, her enthusiasm contagious.

Max smiled.

He took her by the hand and went into the living room. Blake was on the couch still shooting bad people on the video game. Because of Tatter's age, Max half expected to see a TV just as small as the one George had. It wasn't. It was huge. Bigger than the one in Max's living room. It was pretty impressive. Next to the couch, along the wall, George and J.J. leaned over Tatter. The lanky old man sat at a computer desk that was up against the corner, his fingers busy at work on the keyboard.

"No... not that one, Tatter." J.J. said, pointing at the screen. "Click this one. What we're looking for is squid-like."

"Yeah... yeah, yeah," Tatter scoffed, typing away.

Max led Peggy back to the couch.

"So you must be Blake."

Blake nodded, not taking his eyes off of the game. "Yep. That's my name. Don't wear it out."

Max laughed under his breath. *Snap much?*

"Well, Blake... you've been playing the game long enough. Time to change it up. I want to watch a movie."

"But I'm almost to the end," Blake whined.

"That's too bad," Max insisted, taking charge as the adult. He never really dealt with kids much. Never really wanted to either. But right now it felt natural and honestly he appreciated the emotional distraction. "You can beat the game later."

Peggy tugged on Max's shirt. When he looked down she was holding the Shrek DVD.

"Come on..." Blake cried. "I've seen that a dozen times already. Just let me beat the game."

"Tough titty, kid." Max turned off the game.

The screen went black.

"What the hell, man? I was almost there. You could have at least let me save the game first."

"Hey now. Do you talk to your mother with that tone?"

"Yeah, what of it?" Blake tossed the game controller down and crossed his arms.

"No you don't." Peggy stuck her tongue out at her younger brother.

He returned the gesture. "I don't want to watch this stupid movie."

"Well, I tell you what…" Max said, taking the DVD out of the case and placing it into the player. "Once the movie is over, I will let you stay up late to beat the game. We can even get some ice cream."

"You're lying," Blake barked, flopping back in his seat.

"Scout's honor," Max said, pressing play on the movie.

"Scout's what?" Blake asked.

"I want ice cream, too." Peggy smiled, taking a seat on the couch, clearly excited to be watching the movie.

"Okay, how about this…" Max stuck out his little finger. "Pinky promise."

"Okay." Blake lit up, sticking his pinky out, too.

They shook on it and Blake nodded, instantly lost in the Shrek movie. Max stood for a second watching the opening credits. He was instantly drawn from the movie when he heard J.J. speak up.

"Yeah, that one… that's the one I'm talking about. Those are the things that came out of Rose's body when I went into Max's bedroom. They were crawling everywhere."

"Are you sure?" Tatter asked. "If that's them, then we are in big fuckin' trouble."

"Ewww… Mr. Tatter said a bad word." Peggy said, her eyes still glued to the TV.

Peggy was a cute little kid. As much as what she just said was adorable, Max felt his heart sink.

Trouble was the last thing he wanted to hear. Not after all that he had already been through.

When he rounded the couch and made it over to the computer, he had to stand on his tiptoes to see over George's round body. The photo displayed on the screen was exactly what he had seen. Exactly what he had been bitten by. Exactly what he had crushed under his boot.

They were grey things covered in slime that looked very close to a leech, only at the base of the body there were tentacles. The thing's head had no eyes, but it did have a small rounded mouth with several rows of sharp teeth.

If what the internet was saying about them was true, then Tatter was right.

The things that had come out of Paul Stellie and his mother were a hell of a lot more than just trouble.

They were otherworldly.

Standing over his friends at the computer, Max tried to read along as they skimmed the site. But he couldn't focus. All he could hear was the pounding rain outside, his mind imagining each drop as one of those slimy little monsters hitting the ground and slithering off in search of a human host.

SIX

The Topsail Beach pier was taking a beating.

Old man, Ryan C. Perish's kayak had toppled over, and slammed violently against the plank it was tied to. The waves roared, rising with the wind and crashed vigorously. The whitecaps pounded the pier. Wood groaned as it was pushed and pulled by the torrential weather front.

The storm was getting worse.

Sheets of rain poured down from dark gray skies.

Lighting flashed, and if anyone would have been around to see it, Perish's boat would have stuck out like a sore thumb. But the instant the flash of white was gone, so was the prospect of seeing the old man's boat. The thunder that followed bellowed out like the roar of a lion prowling through a deep cavern.

The waters rose and had been doing so for quite some time. The beach front was half the size it had been only hours before, now swallowed up by the forceful ocean waves.

The entire coastline was feeling Tropical Storm Faye's power.

Trees fell apart sending debris through town like scattered confetti.

Houses shook and thunder rumbled.

However, that was just the beginning of the storm.

The rope tied to old man Perish's kayak snapped. The waves were too much for the lifeline. One massive wave rose up and crashed down. The pier groaned in protest as the wood split and bent, giving way under the weight of the monstrous wave.

When the mammoth upsurge of water crashed down, returning to the normal surge of stormy waves, the pier was no longer there.

All that remained was splintered wood floating along the turbulent waves and snapped planks still jutting up from the ocean surface.

Boards and debris littered the beach as the waves drove inland.

The flooding had begun.

*****

Planks of splintered sundried wood weren't the only thing that scattered the sands.

Grayish things the size of a first writhed and squirmed with life. The beach was covered with them for miles, the waves having drawn them up from the ocean depths.

The east coast of the island all the way across town to Surf City was alive with the slithering creatures. With each wave, crashing into the sands came more. They slipped and crawled across the beach, the rain and wind beating down on them like tears from the Heavens.

It didn't take long before their numbers grew, forcing the first wave of sluggish creatures farther inland. They slid through the yards of beachfront property, through the streets beyond, and into the night.

*****

On Elderich Street, Kenny Landon gripped the wheel of his 2006 Ford Ranger. The small truck slid across the wet pavement, barely clinging to the tire's treads.

Kenny was a real estate salesman for the Topsail Beach district. Things had been pretty slow, with more people leaving the area than moving in. That's how retirement spots were. He hated it. In fact, he had been debating on a new career. If it weren't for his wife's job at the hospital in Surf City, they would have been up a creek without a paddle. That was how he felt right now driving through this weather. He squinted his eyes to get a better look past the rain beating down on his windshield, his wipers on full blast. If it got any worse out there, he would literally be up the creek, and a paddle was the last thing he had packed in the truck. At his side were a few three ring binders. The contents of the binders were standard real estate information. Houses for sale. Prime real-estate tips for both commercial and residential properties. The same old stuff.

But one of the folders had something. Something with potential.

With the residential market slow for the area, Kenny had taken out the last of their savings for an investment property. If his wife ever found out, she would probably leave. That was why he was out on the road in this damn storm now. She worked nights at the hospital. If he was going to close on the property and put together a proper slideshow and proposal to use in hopes of gaining her approval, now was the time to do it. He just hoped it would work out. With retirement property came vacation rentals and great getaway spots. That's what Kenny was banking on when he made the $36,000 purchase. Yeah, it was a lot of money, but she would understand once she saw what he planned to do with it.

The truck pulled to a stop and he looked out the driver's side window at the abandoned motel. It was small. Saying it was run down would have been an understatement, which was how he got it so cheap. This was true. But it was beach front property. Had he known the weather was going to get this bad this quick, he would have just gone home. But he had to see the place one last time. To the average person it probably looked like a dump. A place they should have torn down years ago. To him it was more than that. That was because, unlike most people in Topsail, Kenny had vision. He saw the motel for what it could be rather than what it was.

With the key to the front desk office in his hand, Kenny looked down at it longingly. He craned his neck over, and looked toward the battered motel. It was hard to see in the rain, the heavy droplets slammed against his windshield and windows. Even still, he could see the beach on either side of the building.

Prime location for a getaway spot.

With how bad things were getting outside, he was surprised he even made it to the beach. In fact, a lot of Topsail had already started flooding. Because of the storm's intensity, he had already determined he would have to take the long way back home when it was time to leave. The route he had planned to take was already in bad shape, the waters still rising, the flooding in town getting worse. He just hoped like hell that the roads further inland weren't as bad. The last thing he needed was to arrive at home after his wife. There would be hell to pay then, and since he was going to be dropping the big bomb tonight, he needed all the chips on his side.

Get it and get out, he thought. His visit would be quick. He just wanted to go inside, checking things out one last time. See the place with the eyes of ownership.

He gritted his teeth and squeezed the key tight.

"This is it," he breathed, opening the truck door and stepping out.

The rain instantly soaked through his clothing and in the time it took him to climb out and close the door, the binders in the passenger seat were drenched.

He shrugged it off and started trudging toward the motel through the water and rain.

Splashing through the puddles and pulling his coat up over his head, Kenny was oblivious to the small shapes on the ground as he raced across the lot to the front door. The fact that it was dark and raining so hard made the ground look like it was getting pelted from the storm just as much as he was. Had he not been so excited about the new business prospect, he might have noticed something odd.

It wasn't the heavy rain coming down on an already semi-flooded area.

No, the ground was moving.

It was alive.

Kenny reached the cover of the building and shoved the key into the office door. Excited, he unlocked the door and swung it open. He didn't even make the first step in when he heard it.

The squishing slither.

It was loud and all around him. It reminded him of what it might sound like if you squeezed a full tube of toothpaste as tightly as you could. Only the sound was consistent and growing louder.

When he turned and took a look, he gasped.

The sidewalk leading up to the motel was moving, and fast. The ground was covered in slimly gray... *things.*

They headed right toward him.

"What the fuck?" He screamed, falling back into the motel.

He stumbled, landing on his ass in the doorway. When he looked up, trying to close the door, he could see them. The entire parking lot was one mass of gray moving slime. Like ants flooding the hill of a disturbed pile, they moved back and forth crossing one another. The slithering wet sound flooded his ears like static snow.

They just kept sliding closer.

The closest one leaped a few feet into the air at him. With what could have only been teeth, the slimy thing latched onto his shoe. That was when Kenny saw the tentacles. They wrapped around the front of his shoe, the tiny suction cups gripping tightly while teeth burrowed deeper.

Kenny screamed again.

As if his whimpering call were a trumpet of attack, more than a dozen of the little creatures that had reached the doorway leaped out toward him.

Latching to his shoulders, forearms, waist, face, and hands, Kenny felt sharp little teeth burrowing all over his body. He fell back, pulling them off and flailing on the floor as more of the creatures entered the doorway. He grabbed one tightly with his right hand. It felt thick and greasy. As it came away, sharp pain surged through his body. Chunks of flesh and blood splashed out from his check where the monster had been. Kenny scooted back on his ass, yanking another one from his shoulder and tossing it across the room. His heart raced and his mind filled with panic.

He watched as the doorway filled with a gray mass of movement. They were coming in after him.

He forced aside the sharp pain that was all over his body and climbed to his feet.

That was when he did the only thing he knew to do.

Kenny Landon ran.

With his legs in motion, both of his hands yanked and pulled, peeling the slimy little sluggish things from his body. He yanked one from his leg that had started eating into his pants. Another from his forearm. He jumped as he reached the door to get over the pile of creatures making their way into the motel. But he didn't stop there. He just kept on running. The Ranger was in view. He looked down for a moment as he ran across the lot, rain pounding down on him and everything else. He watched as one of those things leaped up to take a bite, but he pulled his hand away just in time. Still, it grabbed hold of his coat and started biting through the fabric. As the truck grew closer, Kenny heard a thunderous sound. It echoed in his head louder than anything he had ever heard before.

When he tripped in a puddle of water, the ground further down than he expected, he stopped screaming. The noise in his head was gone. Before he could get back up, the creatures were on him again. He felt them land all over his back. Felt them biting into him. He looked around as he staggered to his feet. They were all over the place.

The rain fell down around him violently, the wind getting heavier.

Kenny forced himself up and forward. The truck was just right there. He tore his coat free and threw it aside as he staggered toward it.

He could hear them chasing after him. The wet slithering sound wouldn't leave his mind.

Without hesitation, Kenny was there climbing back into the truck. Trying to catch his breath, he turned to close the door.

It was too late.

The sea-slugs flooded the truck like one massive blob of gray muscle. Kenny fell onto the three ring binders, the rain, wind, and tentacle-things swarming him from the open door. He heard the sound of heavy rain as everything went black with pain. Only it wasn't rain he was hearing. It was more of those things outside the truck trying to get in; their slimy little bodies slamming against the truck's metal frame.

The pain was sensory overload for Kenny. He had never felt anything this horrific in all his life. He had gotten third degree burns, broken bones, paper cuts... that's what this was... this was thousands of tiny paper cuts over his entire body. The cuts ate through his clothing. Ate through his flesh. Burrowed deep to the bone with salty suction cup tentacles.

Even against all odds, and all the agony, he lifted his hand reaching for the passenger door. He needed to get out. Get to his wife. Share with her their new business venture. The motel was going to be a success.

Before his fingers ever reached the door handle, he was too far gone, all of his energy spent.

Just before Kenny faded into the nothingness, his attempt to reach the door was replaced by a fleeting twitch. The spasm of his muscles forced his eyes open. It was hard to see past the rain coming down on his windshield. It was even harder to see past the things climbing all over him, eating their way into his body. But what he saw, he knew was real. You would think that in that last most important final moment, no matter how horrifying, peace would overcome you. You would push past the pain and think of your loved ones. Of times you spent doing the things you loved. Of pets and birthdays. Of friends and accomplishments. All of that in a single moment was crushed and Kenny wasn't given the opportunity for pleasant thoughts. What his eyes witnessed was utterly impossible and truly terrifying.

In that instant, lighting flashed over the ocean just past the motel off to the left of the building.

The mountain covered in eyes that was making its way out of the sea didn't matter.

Kenny Landon was dead.

SEVEN

Back at Tatter Drake'o's place things were getting pretty interesting.

J.J., although still technically on duty, was on his eighth beer. The kitchen refrigerator had been emptied of adult beverages. Experience had taught the young police officer that Tatter kept a backup supply in the garage refrigerator. Max had taken a seat on the arm of the couch while watching J.J. staggering back and forth with his drink. J.J. slurred his words. The only reason why Max could make out what the cop had been saying was because he had been on repeat since beer five. '*I kill...ed people tonight. Can you... huk... believe it? I just shot them, like that, right in the... face. I killed people tonight*'.

The movie Shrek was already more than thirty minutes in and Peggy was grinning ear to ear. On the other hand, Blake was slouched on the couch wearing an expression of indifference. Still, it was obvious to Max that the young boy had long forgotten about beating his video game. Two completely demolished bowls of ice cream sat on the coffee table in front of the couch, the kids quiet and content.

George Braidy sat beside Tatter with his arms crossed. Tatter remained hunched over the computer. The contents of the website *Bizarro World* scrolled across the screen with headlines like Alien visitors from Pluto, Killer koala bears from another dimension, and FBI cover-ups.

"Bunch of hogwash if you ask me," George scolded, spitting tobacco juice into his empty beer bottle.

"Nobody asked you, old fat man."

"Oh, so I'm old '*and*' fat now, Tatter? Look whose talkin'." George barked, accenting the word 'and' with a long draw.

"Hey, I just calls 'em like I sees 'em." Tatter chuckled, not taking his eyes off the computer screen.

Max Willgood stood with his legs together, leaning against the arm rest of the couch. He stared down blankly at the warm beer in his hand. Sipping on it hadn't done a thing for him. He just didn't want it. Didn't want to drown his sorrows. Not yet. He needed to keep it together. If not for himself, then for J.J.'s sake. The cop had lost it. Watching him get drunk and stumble around the living room was enough to keep Max from following suit.

Max looked up from the beer and glanced at George, who returned the gesture. It was as if they were both thinking the same thing. Only, Max knew better. The old man wasn't even close to thinking the same thing. All Max could think about was how stupid it had been to come here. His wife was dead and lying in his living room and here they were looking up Big Foot's address because the cookie monster wanted to send him a ticket to the loony bin concert. J.J.'s current state was just icing on the cake. He watched the intoxicated officer shamble across the living room again, pacing back and forth as he mumbled. Max's eyes looked down at the cuffs on the cop's belt. That made him think of the keys to the cuffs, which in turn made him think of the patrol car keys tucked away in the drunk's front pocket. As J.J. turned around, starting his pace across the room again from the other side, Max watched the keys in the officer's front pocket bulge with each step. If George had any sense left he would be ready to get in that cop car and leave the moment Max built up the courage to snatch those keys right out of J.J.'s pocket.

Max stared back down at the beer in his hand, started to bring it to his mouth, but didn't. The warm smell made his stomach churn. He suddenly felt weak and wasn't sure if he wanted to make a move for the keys or lie down to take a nap. The severity of the situation suddenly hit him like a fat sack of bricks. A nap would fix that. He took a deep breath and sighed to keep the tears from surfacing.

Just when he started to take a deep breath again and make for the keys, Tatter spoke up.

"Check this shit out, guys."

"Ewwww…" Peggy chuckled. "Mister Tatter said a ba—"

"Check this '*stuff*' out… I mean." Tatter corrected himself, smiling at the little girl.

"What'cha got?" George asked.

"Well…" Tatter cleared his throat, squinting at the screen with those thick framed glasses. "That thing you seen, those squid-things that attacked Max, they're called *Cephan…eeesoo*." His pronunciation was drawn and long.

"Ceph-a-what?" Max asked, putting the beer down next to Peggy's empty bowl of ice cream and walking over to the computer to have a look for himself.

"Cephanisio," Tatter said, this time a little more confident with his wording. "I think that's how you say it."

"What are they?" Max scratched his mustache, thinking for a moment of his wife's distaste in facial hair.

"Well, it says here that they're a member of the squid family just like you said."

"Hell, man," Max said, pointing at the photo on the monitor. "What else could they be? Bunch a legs. Suction cups. But that just doesn't make much sense. I have never seen a single squid with a head like that. Those teeth."

"That ain't no shit," George muttered from his stoop. Max heard spit leave the large man's mouth and then he continued. "Mother-fuckers done eat a hole right out of them people. Like it were nothin'. Then that woman… how'd she get back up like—"

"I'm getting' to that. Keep your shorts on, fat man." Tatter swung a limp wrist in his direction. "This creature is a member of the superorder Decapodiformes from the Greek for… bla, bla, bla…" Tatter said, reading the site information. "Like all cephalopods, squid have complex digestive systems. The muscular stomach is found roughly in the midpoint of the visceral mass. From there, the bolus moves into the… bla, bla, bla…" He skimmed farther down. "Okay, here we go. This is what we're looking for. A loose pantheon of ancient, powerful deities from space who once ruled the Earth and who have since fallen into a deathlike sleep were once feared by man. Forced into the deep by a—"

"What the fuck are you reading?" Max scoffed. "We're talking about real squids that did a lot of damage. Killed my wife. Not something from the movie Ghost Busters."

"Look, man." Tatter threw his hands up. "I didn't ask you guys to come over. The front door is right over there. Be my guest."

Max took a deep breath, and glared toward the door. When he looked at George, the old man shook his head, nodding toward Tatter to continue.

"And besides," Tatter demanded. "This ain't my website. I'm not the one who posted this stuff."

"Whatever," Max barked. "Are we really going to sit here and listen to this crap, George? We need to go."

"Just give him a minute, Max. I know it sounds crazy, but you have to admit that what happened tonight was crazy. Besides…I already know where this is going."

"You do?" Max sagged back onto the couch arm. "What do you mean?"

"Tatter's talking about the Old Ones. Or well, the old *one*."

"That's right," Tatter said, leaning back at the desk. He adjusted his bottle cap glasses and said, "The old ones, man. I knew they were real. I just knew it!"

George took a deep breath, reached into his mouth with two fingers and pulled out the chew. Stuffing it into the bottle he had been holding, he set it aside and stood to his feet. The room fell silent while he reached into the back of his pants and grabbed the dip for a fresh pinch. The soundtrack from Shrek played in the background.

Peggy was wide eyed and glued to the television. Blake had already fallen asleep sitting upright on the couch. Drool dripped drown from his cheek onto his shoulder, and his head bobbed left to right on occasion. The rain outside was still giving it hell and the wind factor had grown bad enough that one of the trees close to Tatter's house beat against the roof with a steady dull drum.

Stuffing the chew in his mouth, George sat back down. "Have you heard of Operation Bumble Bee, Max?"

"It's about to get thick in here." Tatter smiled, rubbing his hands together with excitement.

"No... should I have?" Max asked, turning to lock eyes with both of them.

"Well, not necessarily," Tatter said. "It all started back whe—"

"Excuse me, Tatter," George said, between dip filled lips. "I think I was the one telling this story."

Tatter closed his mouth to let the old man continue.

And he did.

Spitting into his glass, he said, "Operation Bumblebee was the U.S. Navy's secret guided missile testing program that operated on Topsail Island from 1946 to 1948."

"Oh, you're talking about that museum just before you get to the bridge into Surf City? Hanna and I went there like a month after we moved here. That place was pretty cool. Bunch of old history."

"That's the place all right," Tatter chimed in with that same wide smile from the photo on the fridge.

"Will you guys be quiet?" Peggy insisted, her index finger to her lips. "I can't hear the movie."

Tatter laughed, mimicking the girl's gesture with a finger to his lips. "Okay, we'll take it to the kitchen."

"Good," she said emphatically. "The good part is about to come up. Shrek is gonna get mad. He's funny when he gets mad."

Tatter motioned to the kitchen. That was when Max noticed J.J. wasn't with them in the living room anymore.

"Hey… did you see where J.J. went?"

"The kitchen, maybe…" George said, following Tatter and Max.

He wasn't there.

He wasn't anywhere. He wasn't in the bathroom or either of the spare bedrooms. The garage was empty, too.

Before Max could ask where he had gone, the patrol car siren engaged. Blue and red light spun against the windows in the kitchen.

"Shit…" Tatter breathed, looking out the window. "J.J.'s in the cruiser."

"Don't let him drive off!" Max hissed. "He was pretty freaking pickled, not to mention the storm. It was hell getting over here as it was. Besides, he's my fucking ride!"

"What the hell does he think he's doing?" George asked.

"Fucked if I know," Tatter said, making for the door.

It was too late. By the time they all stepped out onto the porch, the cruiser was gone. The rain beat down from outside, the wind blowing hard and heavy.

"Close the door," Blake said, now standing beside Max. He rubbed the sleep from his eyes and pulled on Max's arm. "When the movie is over do I still get to beat my game?"

"I… I…" Max looked down at the kid, back at the door and J.J.'s missing car, then back at the boy again. "I don't know. I just want to go home and get some sleep. You look like you could use some sleep, too." His words were dust against his lips as they fluttered from the back of his throat.

"But I'm not sleepy." Blake sighed with one massive yawn. "I'm not tired at all, I swear."

EIGHT

"What are we going to do about J.J.?"

"What do you mean, what are we goin'a do?" Tatter shrugged. "J.J.'ll be fine. This ain't his first rodeo. I mean, his first time to leave here pickled. The kid's been worse off before truckin' it back to his place. If he gets pulled over by another cop, I doubt he'll get anything more than a slap on the wrist."

"Yeah…" Max said, pointing toward the living room from where he stood in the kitchen. Shifting his weight from one foot to the other, he said, "But in this weather… and with those things out there?"

"What? The killer squids from another world?" Tatter laughed. "I know you all came over here to pull my leg… and you got me good. I'll give you that." He pointed his long slender finger at the fat man. "But, boy, don't play me. I know I need to lay off the conspiracy sites and get back to the real world. So just drop it, okay?" Tatter patted George on the shoulder.

However, when Max's nor George's weary face didn't falter Tatter's grin subsided, replaced with dread. "Fuck-me-runnin'." He looked to George, who wore that same cold glare on his face. "You guys really are serious."

"I'm afraid so, Tatter," George mumbled, despairingly.

The kitchen fell silent.

"Well, then…" Tatter stared at the floor, took off his glasses and proceeded to wipe them on his dirty shirt. "What am I supposed to do about it, then?"

"You can start off by telling the boy about the museum."

"Oh, yeah…" Tatter said, putting his glasses back on.

Max paced across the kitchen to the window above the sink. He pulled the curtain back and looked outside. The rain came down heavy through the bleak and dark night. He shook his head with distaste and turned to Tatter.

"No offense, but I don't think fairy tales are going to do much right now," Max said. "What we need is to borrow your car and go to the station. Obviously, someone has tried to communicate with the paramedics or that cop back at my house. They'll be out looking for them. Something… We need to act. I owe it to Hanna to do… something."

"Max is right," George agreed, wiping his clammy hands on his big belly.

"But I got the kids here with me. I can't go anywhere—not in this weather."

"We're not asking you to go with us. I just need to borrow the car. We'll get it back to you. I promise."

Tatter stood there a second, considering things.

"Well?"

"All right." Tatter threw his hands up. "You can borrow the car. But before you go, I think you need to hear the rest of the story. George is right about that much. If this shit is real, it's pretty fucked up stuff. Even I don't believe half of it… sometimes."

Max nodded. The three men took a seat at the bar.

Tatter told him everything about the Old Ones. With George adding snippets of information here and there to fill in the blanks, Max sat listening to the obscene story.

According to the two old men, everyone in Topsail Beach knew about Operation Bumblebee. It was the town's one sour stain in the history books. A past that couldn't be covered no matter how much tourism flooded the beach every season. Every town had one bad story, Operation Bumblebee was theirs.

"These Old Ones were a loose pantheon of ancient, powerful deities from space who once ruled the Earth. They have since fallen into a deathlike sleep."

What that had to do with the little squid-like-things, Tatter could only speculate based off what the website mentioned. But what they did know was why the museum had been built in the first place.

"It hadn't always been a museum," Tatter continued. "But, had in fact been the testing grounds for missile research. At least that's what the government wants the world and the good ole people of Topsail Island to believe. Operation Bumblebee was a staging ground for astrological research. The stars, kid. Yes, they did make many nuclear and biometric breakthroughs in the field of neuroscience. Even played a major role in the cold war and helped see World War II to the end. The missile development was out of this world. They invented major elements of what today is known as chemical warfare, which is why they got that museum up. All them old missiles and what not. But still, that's just them coverin' the truth."

"All of that was just the cover," George butted in. "The real reason behind the operation was the buildings location in conjunction to our solar system. Communication—literally beyond our world."

"Wait a second," Max said. "If they covered all of that stuff up, then how do you two know about it?"

"Everybody does, kid," Tatter said. "You know how long ago the cold war was? Think about it. Over the years people forget. They chose to forget. Get paid to forget. Downright stop believing it. Generations later, it all becomes myth. Folklore. No one talks about it anymore because it just seems too silly to be true."

"That ain't no shit," George said, laughing. "I can't say as I ever believed any of it, but I still heard all the stories just the same."

"Yeah, but how does this Bumble-whatever have anything to do with what happened at my house?"

"Those squid-fuckers," Tatter said, nodding. "The Bizarro World site of mine suggests those things are somehow tied to the Old Ones. Parasites… leeches that form from her body and break away, multiplying like rabbits. If that's the case, then she's awake."

"She?"

"The last time she woke it was contained. Never got any further than the beach."

Just when Max was about to give up on both the old men and tell them they were both loons, Peggy stepped into the kitchen. Her eyes were heavy, both fists pressing into them as she yawned. Her Miss Piggy shirt was wrinkled and her hair a mess.

"I fell asleep…" she breathed. "The movie's over and Blake is taking up the couch." Her voice was soft and sweet.

Max's heart sank as he looked down on her. She reminded him so much of Hanna. Thinking on it now, what had happened back at the house had somehow already seemed like years ago. And still, it was surreal. Unreal even. His wife was at home right now laughing with the neighbors about the terrible joke they had all played on him. Max knew that wasn't true, but he wanted it to be.

"It is getting pretty late," Tatter said, looking at the big fish clock beside the refrigerator. "Come on, Peggy. Let's get you and Blake off to bed."

Tatter nodded toward his two guests and went into the living room to wake up Blake. With both children on their feet, he took them to one of the guest bedrooms. When he returned, he seemed sad. Worried. Like something beyond what had already transpired tonight was amiss.

"What's up?"

"The kids…" he said, eyeing the clock. "Their mom should-a been back by now to take them home. It's already nearly midnight. That's not like her. If she were gonna snag a few extra hours, she would a called."

"Well, that ain't no good." George sighed. "Think them things got'er? With how much those things were multiplyin' they could be all over town by now."

"Do you have a number to call her on?"

Tatter nodded and went to the phone. Dialing the number from memory, he waited.

"Shit…"

"What?"

"The phone… the line is dead."

"Here…" Max said. "Use my cellphone." He retrieved it from his front pocket and handed it to the tall skinny fisherman. "Maybe the wind knocked down a phone line or something."

"I guess," Tatter agreed, taking the phone. He dialed the number and held the device to his ear. "It's ringing."

George and Max nodded happily.

However, that is all it did. The phone rang and rang. No one answered. No voicemail. No nothing. Just the busy *ring, ring, ring.*

"No good," Tatter sighed, handing back the phone. Max pocketed it and shrugged.

"What are we going to do?"

"I don't plan to do nothin', Max," Tatter stated. "I can't take the kids out in that weather. I'm just gonna hunker down and wait till their mom gets home."

"If… she comes home," Max said.

"That ain't no shit!"

"Look, guys, I don't need this negativity. I get enough of that at the pub." Tatter riffled through his overalls and fetched his car keys. "If you two plan on headin' toward the station, I got one request."

"Check on Patty at the diner?"

"You bet'cha," Tatter said smiling.

"I think we can manage," George agreed. "The diner ain't that far from the station. We need to get there and let someone know what's goin' on."

Finally, Max thought, *George is thinking with his head. That's where we should have gone in the first place.* He took a deep breath and felt an invisible weight lift from his shoulders. They were finally doing something sensible. Max and George said their goodbyes and stepped out onto the porch headed toward Tatter's car.

The instant the rain and wind came down around them, the heavy sunken dread returned.

Thunder crashed, followed by a flash of lighting. The darkness lit up in a bright hue of white for a moment and then faded, making it harder to see than before. Max's eyes had to readjust. The drops of rain were heavy and cold. They sent chills up his body as they trudged through the flooding yard. The water soaked through his shoes and socks quickly. His eyes darted back and forth in the rain for any sign of those… *those things*.

When he looked up at George, he could tell that the bulbous man was doing the same.

They were both on high alert, their nerves already shot.

Something terrible brewed in the night. And it wasn't the storm.

They both climbed into Tatter's rusted out car. The thing was so old and had so many dents in it that Max couldn't tell what kind of car it was. Whatever it was, it was old. And old cars were unreliable. Max had helped out many people in the area with automotive repair. It was something his employer would have frowned upon had they found out he was doing it on the side for extra money. He'd completely rebuilt George's motor, and even changed the radiator on Ms. Stellie's car. But Tatter's junk bucket on wheels—Max had never seen the thing. Didn't even realize the skinny old man had one. He had only seen Tatter at the pier fishing or at the bar downing drinks and telling stories. The lanky man was more of a walker, since he lived so close to the beach and the pub left no need for wheels. Hell, had Max known he had a car, he probably would have turned down the offer for extra cash in return for fixing the thing up. The sight of it screamed 'lost cause' to Max and he gritted his teeth hoping with all he had that the damn thing would turn over when he turned the key in the ignition. Having slid into the driver's seat, he twisted the key. The engine sputtered and spit. He turned the key again, this time giving it gas. He pumped the pedal twice. A third and fourth time. The engine roared to life. Well, not so much to life. Life in a car sounded warm and consistent like a cat's purr. This was more like the drowning squeal of a raccoon caught in a sack. It thumped and sputtered. Once Max backed out of the driveway and started down the road, the engine seemed to level out.

They drove through the neighborhood and took one right turn, then a left. That put them on one of the main streets heading toward the Surf City Bridge. On any normal night, they would be there in fifteen minutes. Now, with the storm surging all around them, the wind pushing the car from side to side, and the rain making it almost impossible to see, there was no telling how long it would take.

The rain came down in sheets.

The wipers on full blast didn't make any difference. It was so bad out there that turning the headlights on bright only made it harder to see. Max squinted, hugging the steering wheel. Aside from the rain pounding against the windshield, the only thing he could see was the white lines in the road. Even that wasn't but a few feet in front of the hood of the car.

"Take it easy," George cautioned.

"I am…" Max replied, looking down at the speedometer. "I'm not even going thirty, man. This rain needs to let up and soon."

Just then, the car dipped hard, the right tires slogging through a large puddle in the road. The water splashed up high and came down hard on the windows.

"That ain't no—"

"Shit!" Max cut him off.

He turned the wheel sharply barely avoiding a head on collision with a parked car that was for no apparent reason just sitting idle in the middle of the street. Max looked in the rearview mirror watching the car behind them get farther away as they drove on.

"That was close."

That was the last thing either one of them said for a few minutes. They just drove on, inching their way closer to town, the rain and winds forcing them to take it slowly.

"You think J.J.'s okay?" Max finally asked, breaking the silence. His voice was distant, almost a whisper, the concern sincere.

"What? That young punk?" George chuckled.

Max knew that laugh all too well. That was the type of laugh George only did when he was nervous.

"He's fine. Like Tatter said, he drives under the bottle all the time. He knows his limits. If he felt like he couldn't drive, I don't think he would a got behind the wheel," George said.

"But the storm, George?" Max insisted. "The wind is blowing too damn hard and I'm having a helluva time just keeping us on the road. And I haven't had anything to drink. I'm really worried about him."

"Me, too," George breathed. "I'm worried about all of us."

NINE

J.J. swerved for the hundredth time, the road weaving back and forth under him like the crashing waves of an endless ocean. He compensated with the wheel, bringing the patrol car back toward the center of the lane.

He needed to focus but couldn't.

He was intoxicated and he knew it.

But he didn't give a flying fuck.

Yet, that wasn't what made it hard to focus on the road as his patrol car zigged and zagged through Tatter's neighborhood. It was what had happened earlier that night. It was messing with his mind. He wasn't prepared for something like that. It had been a question he asked himself constantly. When he decided he wanted to become an officer, following in his grandfather's footsteps, he asked himself if he could handle the stress and strain of the job. His granddad had told him countless stories of on the job trauma. Ten car pile-ups. Drug overdose victims. The violence. The death. His favorite story told by his dad's old man had been the one and only time he had actually shot and killed someone. A burglar caught in the act lunged out with a knife and got shot in the process. It was his gramps that had pulled the trigger. As a teen those stories excited him. Made him want to do those kinds of things. Made him want to experience them. The adrenaline got his veins pumping each time the stories were told. It made him feel alive. Invigorated. After high school he asked himself that question again when he actually enlisted into the academy. The answer, he felt, was that he could in fact handle it. Silly thing was, nothing ever happened in Topsail, which was what led to the drinking habit; boredom. And here he was now, buckling like a cowardly little girl. Tears running down his cheeks. The memory of shooting a fellow officer and two paramedics flashed in constant repeat in his mind.

His hands shook.

The steering wheel tried to veer hard left and he jerked right to realign the car on the road. His vision was blurred from the beers and as he slowed the car down to look around, he wasn't exactly sure what part of the neighborhood he was in. Surely, he had to be close to Tatter's house.

But what did it matter?

He was a murderer. His nerves locked up and he felt sick to his stomach. His insides gritted and groaned with every flash of violence playing in his mind. His stomach was in his chest now trying to rise up.

He slowed the cruiser to a dead crawl to ease his nausea and looked around, trying to assess his exact location. He had to be somewhere between Alabama Avenue and 5th street, which would put him only a few blocks from Tatter's and closer to the beachfront. He knew this because between blurred eyes he could make out the fire hydrant in front of Miss Chestnut's house. It was a landmark in the neighborhood because it wasn't red like most fire hydrants. This one was actually painted like a Dalmatian—white with black spots.

Stupid thing, he thought while looking at the fire hydrant.

At least he knew where he was.

He took a deep breath, rolled to a complete stop, and put the cruiser in park.

The rain came down so hard that the neighborhood seemed unusually dark. Normally the area would be lit up by the night stars and glowing gray moon. Tonight there was none of that. Just doom-filled clouds raining down their tears. That was how he felt; doomed and ready to cry. Maybe crying would make him feel better about what had happened. It wasn't his fault after all. He was only doing what was right. Acting on the simple motor functions of natural instinct. If anything, he had saved Max and George. That had to be worth something.

His stomach settled, the sickness subsided.

He was parked in front of Miss Chestnut's house, a two story legacy of what was called old money. Her descendants from way back had been wealthy enough that J.J. was sure he hadn't seen the woman work a single day in her life. All the other homes on the block were small one story houses cookie cut from the same mold. Ahead of him about a block or so up was the neighborhood playground. There was only one basketball goal for those not fortunate enough for a full court game. A few feeble swings and a couple of benches, but that was about it.

Although the park was far enough off that he couldn't see it, J.J. thought about it for a moment—remembering how many times he and Tatter would have a shit load of drinks and walk over and shoot hoops. Mostly two games of Horse. Tatter wasn't much of a runner and J.J. didn't blame him. Neither was he.

A sudden flash of light engulfed the sky and vanished just as fast.

The loud thunderous *boom* that roared in its wake forced the sickening sensations back to the surface. At the same instant the thunder bellowed out, J.J.'s mind flashed back to Max's yard, the trigger of his 9mm being pulled and Markus Gunther's brain spraying out the back side. Dead. Mark was dead. Just like that. They had been friends in high school. Been to one another's homes. Enjoyed small talk at the station. Had each other's backs on the job countless times. They knew each other. They were… friends. And J.J. shot him without thought.

How could I…

J.J.'s stomach churned.

That was when he threw up.

Chunks of vomit splashed across the steering wheel, the smell of warm beer permeating the car's interior instantly.

"Fuckin' pathetic," J.J. breathed, wiping his mouth with his sleeve.

When those words left his mouth he began to sob.

It was as if he hadn't said them. It was almost as if his granddad has spoken them through him. He was a disappointment. A failure. A fuck up. What kind of cop got drunk three nights a week with the town's crazy man and drove home each night intoxicated? What type of cop loses his shit after killing someone? A pussy… that's what kind of a cop he was. He was a disgrace. A shame to his heritage. He had gone into law enforcement to honor his grandfather and here he was fucking it up. Losing his cool. If the old man were here to see him now, he just knew he would laugh at him. Be told to pony up and be a real man. That's all he had ever tried to be. He just couldn't hack it.

The truth hit him dead center in the chest like a soggy sack of nickels. He hadn't been ready for the stress of the job, the question after all that time finally answered.

J.J. slammed his fist into the steering wheel.

Anger boiled inside, forcing the sick feeling to dissipate. How could he be so weak?

Thunder crashed in the distance again.

He took a deep breath, his chest jittering nervously as he inhaled. In one fluid motion, he wiped the tears and leftover vomit from his cheek.

He reached for his holster retrieving the 9mm. It felt different in his hands now that he had killed someone with it. A weapon of death more than just something you used for target practice at the range. No, it wasn't just for penetrating cardboard cutouts of a stereotypical assailant. It was much more than that now. The weapon felt cold and heavy in his quivering palm. It was death.

It called to him.

It needed him.

He could end this now. End the shame that had fallen upon his family name. He was a waste. A mess. Unprepared. A let down. His granddad was probably in Heaven now looking down on him with disgust. He was covered in vomit and shaking like a little girl, all because he didn't have it in him.

He cocked the pistol and lifted it.

His eyes focused on the barrel as he aimed it toward his face. The weapon blurred in and out of focus as J.J. squinted with drunken eyes trying to see it.

"Just do it, you worthless fuck," he spat, coaxing himself to pull the trigger.

The tears flowed anew as he thought of Markus and the two paramedics. They had families. Kids and parents. Pets and futures. Birthdays and Christmases to look forward to. Not anymore. He had taken that away from them.

He dropped the gun in his lap, the sobs flowing heavier now, like the rain that beat down against his windshield.

He couldn't bring himself to do it.

He wasn't his grandfather.

He didn't have what it took… what it took to be a real man.

This was just too much.

He stared down at the gun, wiping snot from his nose. Maybe this was being a real man. Just because Granddad had told the stories with bravery didn't mean he was brave in the moment. Everything at Max's house had transpired so quickly. It could all just be—

Someone screamed.

When he looked up, he couldn't see anything. Just the rain beating down against the windshield.

The scream came again. This time closer—female.

J.J. strained to see beyond the murky dark weather beaten street ahead. A flourish spray of circling red and blue light helped light up the night around him. That was when the haze of his drunken mind realized the cruiser lights was still engaged. He reached down, fumbling for the switch to turn them off.

Thump!

The driver's side window rocked hard sending J.J. out of his seat. The sudden startle made him bite his tongue. He felt warm iron-filled blood fill his mouth. When he swallowed, looking up, his heart plunged in dread. The woman standing at the cruiser door, beating on the window, was covered in muck. She was drenched from head to toe in rain water, the rain still steadily coming down all around her. Her long brown hair was pulled straight by the weight of the rain, her clothing clung tightly and wet to her body. She was panicked and out of breath. Her skin was pale and her shirt… her shirt was covered in something brown or maybe black.

Blood.

The woman was covered in blood.

J.J. focused on her features for a moment and then realized who it was. It was Blake and Peggy's mom. She was still wearing her work uniform from the diner. The slender black slacks. The striped gold and red shirt with black tie. The nametag just above her right breast.

She screamed, beating against the window, her words muffled between the thick glass of the window.

Realizing what he was about to do with the gun resting in his lap, J.J. shook his head.

Suicide, really?

He shook his head and took a deep breath. With the sobering moment came the taste of acidic beer filled lungs, the back of his throat still ripe with the remnant chunks of spew.

"What the hell's going on?" he demanded while cracking the window. Even to himself, his voice seemed more stern and in control than he had expected. No slur of intoxication. No panic or stress. Just control and readiness. He thought about that while, wondering if she could smell the beer wafting off of him from within the cruiser.

"Oh, dear God!" she screamed, oblivious to his intoxicated state. Her eyes were wide with fear, her body trembling and wet. "There's been an accident just up the road! I ran over someone!"

"Calm down, ma'am," J.J. insisted, trying to open the car door and step out. She wouldn't move from her spot, which prevented him from getting out.

"No... J.J., I can't!" she cried. Now J.J. felt like an ass, because she knew his name but he couldn't for the life of him remember hers. "I was on my way to Tatter's to get the kids and someone ran out in front of me. I didn't see them in time. When I got out to help, they attacked me. Scratched me all up. Tried to bite me!"

J.J. looked down at her arms. They were covered in deep lacerations. The blood ran down them amidst the falling rain running down her skin.

"And then..." her voice trembled with fear. "Candy Hines, the lady that lives just on the other side of the playground. She came out of her house to help. Heard the accident from inside. The person I hit. They… they attacked her. They were eating her, J.J.! Oh, dear God." Her voice trailed off.

J.J. suddenly felt tense as the panic and stress of the situation pumped adrenaline through his body at more than ninety miles a minute. His vision became focused. Clear. Even after downing that much alcohol he knew what to do.

He needed to act. Be the man in charge. Be the person his grandfather expected him to be.

"Step aside, Patty," he said, very matter-of-fact. He opened the door and climbed out the cruiser, happy he remembered her name. The fact that it was on her nametag was a dead giveaway, but that was beside the point. He holstered the pistol, closed the door, and said "Here… I'm going to let you sit in the back of the cruiser while I go investigate."

He opened the back driver's side door ushering her inside.

"Shouldn't you call someone?" she muttered, climbing into the back seat.

"Shit…" J.J. breathed, having forgotten protocol. Maybe the alcohol still impaired his judgment. Shutting her door and climbing back into the patrol car, he radioed dispatch.

No one answered.

There was only white noise.

"Fuck…" He gritted his teeth, placing the receiver back down.

Stepping out the car, he glanced at Patty with a quick nod and was off to face the horrors awaiting him.

The question that played in his mind with each trudging step through the rain filled street was one and the same.

Do I have what it takes?

TEN

With one foot in front of the other, his feet splashed through the growing puddles in the street. It wasn't until he was up and walking again that he realized how drunk he really was. His head spun and his surroundings tried to fall out from under him. He shook it off after taking a deep breath, the 9mm gripped tightly in both hands, the safety on.

When he looked back at the patrol car, he was surprised how far he had already jogged. He had less than half a block to go before he would be at the park.

No sign of the accident, yet. Aside from the heavy rain falling around him, the night was silent.

With each splashing step toward the park, J.J gritted his teeth while reflecting on his life.

How could things have gotten this bad?

Just when he was about to internally chew himself a new asshole for even thinking about pointing a gun to his head, the accident came into view. There was Patty's car... and that sound. The wet slurping, grunting hiss of satisfaction.

His heart pounded and his fists gripped tighter on the pistol.

Patty drove a dark blue compact family van. It was parked in the middle of the street. Nothing out of place about it, really. Walking up to the vehicle, all he could see was its rear. The headlights were still on, and he heard the motor running as he got closer. Rain pounded against the hood, splashing down around it to the asphalt. The park was to his right. None of the park's lights were on because it was technically closed after 9pm, but even with the rain coming down as hard as it was, he could see the silhouette of the lone basketball goal. Beyond that were some swings and a large slide, but they were too far off in the darkness to see.

As he rounded the family van, he saw two legs sprawled out across the pavement. Each limb jittered slightly in place.

"Fuck..." he breathed, switching the safety off on his pistol.

Taking each step with caution, J.J. tried to reach the front of the van in silence. It was useless. His soggy boots sloshed and squeaked with each step. To him they were the loudest thing he had ever heard—though that wasn't true.

He cringed as the figure came into view.

The man, or what looked like a man, was kneeling over Ms. Hines; the woman who lived across from the park. The man was on his knees and had his back to J.J. He was doing something to her. J.J. knew exactly what it was. The wet slurping grunts registered in his mind like a ticking time bomb.

J.J. walked right up behind the man and aimed the pistol at him. His hands shook. The gun felt heavier than he had remembered. It was slippery, the rain soaking through his hands to the grip.

"Freeze!" J.J. shouted, his voice wavering.

The man didn't respond. He just remained over Ms. Hines slurping and grunting.

"I... I said, *FREEZE!*" J.J. shouted with confidence, jamming the gun toward the figure.

J.J. sidestepped to get a better look at Ms. Hines. When he did, he instantly wished he hadn't. Her face was gone. Just gone. All that remained was a splotch of red running goop, her attacker digging into it with his hand. Pulling the meaty red substance away, the man brought it to his mouth. The blood and meat shone with glistening wetness as J.J. watched him begin to chew. The man's face was smeared with gore, his hands caked with chunks of torn skin and flesh.

J.J.'s eyes darted back the way he had come and then back to the man eating Ms. Hines. The patrol car was no long in view. All he could see was darkness and the rain coming down around it. He needed to call for backup. There was just no way he could handle this alone. Not after what had already happened. The thought of pulling the trigger on this man, right here and now, flashed through his head. He couldn't do it. He needed to try reasoning with him.

However, for some reason J.J. knew it wasn't going to work.

"Put your hands on top of your head and turn around, now!" J.J. demanded, his finger floating over the trigger.

The man still didn't respond.

That was when instinct took over for J.J.

It was almost as if his body was no longer his, and the man his granddad had wanted him to be just stepped in to take over.

J.J. watched as the events transpired; shocked any of it was happening at all.

He stepped forward with two long strides and kicked the man as hard as he could in the back.

"I said, fuckin' freeze!" The words rolled out into the air from J.J.'s lips as if a ventriloquist had said them for him.

The man slumped to the asphalt beside Ms. Hines and turned.

The full magnitude of the situation rolled across J.J.'s eyes like a radioactive filter of horror. His eyes burned at the horrid sight. Ms. Hines lay motionless on the road, her legs still twitching. Not only had her face been torn clean off, but her blouse had been ripped away revealing what was left of her midsection and breasts. They were minced meat and mangled pulp. Strings of intestine draped across her torso and onto the street. The puddle forming around her was a mixture of rain water and blood.

The memory of his grandfather's expectations and the thought of self-loathing instantly vanished in the wake of the devastating sight.

The man on the ground looked up at J.J. and hissed. Up until that moment, J.J. had honestly forgotten about him—lost in the horrors committed to Ms. Hines' body.

J.J. jumped to attention and pointed the 9mm at the man.

The man started to stand, hissing and covered in blood. Meat fell from his lips down to the cement as he snarled wildly showing red-stained teeth.

"I said freeze!" J.J. screamed, his voice shaking just as much as the pistol.

The man lunged forward with both hands out and his mouth wide.

J.J. pulled the trigger.

The loud report bellowed through the neighborhood. J.J. watched the man fall awkwardly, landing to his back on the wet pavement. The headlights on Patty's family van illuminated the scene as the man lay motionless on the ground, blood pooling around the gunshot wound in his chest.

Startled, the officer stood there a moment, the gun still aimed at its target.

The target did not move.

He studied the man for a moment and recognized the hole in the center of his throat. It was the same as the ones he had seen back at Max's house. It seeped black and red fluid like thick syrupy sludge. More than that, he recognized the man. It was Scotty Watts. Scotty lived only a few blocks over, closer to the water. He was in his late twenties, worked at the local video store, and generally closed up at night. He was even still wearing his blue *Blockbuster* work shirt. It was covered in Ms. Hines' blood and meaty insides. With the rise of Redbox and Netflix, the place he worked at was close to going out of business. Still, Scott stuck around waiting things out. That's just how Scotty was. He was a good man. Worked hard. Played hard. Loyal. Had a cute girlfriend and even had a damn good pitching arm. He wasn't a killer. Sure, he was into scary movies like anyone else his age... but this... this Hannibal Lector crap, that wasn't him. He wasn't crazy. He wasn't a murderer and he sure as hell didn't eat people. He was normal just like everyone else in town.

What the hell is happening in Topsail? J.J. thought, studying the dense cavity in Scotty's throat.

Then J.J. saw it squirm.

Not on Scotty, but on Ms. Hines. The gray, greasy little creature slithered across her arm and up her chest. J.J. stood frozen in wonder and reflected on things he had seen over at Max's place. He watched it stop at her throat, burrowing deep into her skin. The creature punctured through with ease, making her neck seem as if it were made of damp paper.

Then the thing was gone.

Neither of the bodies moved.

The rain poured. J.J. was drenched to the bone after having only been in the weather for a few minutes.

He scanned the darkness beyond Patty's blue family van. Nothing seemed out of place. The neighborhood—or at least what little of it he could see past the rain—seemed quiet.

The wind picked up, blowing back toward the cruiser, which reminded him that Patty was still sitting in the back seat. He needed to attend to her and see about reaching someone on the CB. The wind blew the rain sideways, stinging him in the eyes. Then the smell came. It slapped him like his ex-girlfriend had done; hard and for no real reason. The stench burned at the back of his throat, making him forget about the acidic vomit taste from earlier. It was sour and salty like something from the ocean. Only it smelled dead. He thought of the last time he and Tatter had been out on the pier fishing all morning. All they could seem to catch were small bait fish. By midday they had given up and just sat back drinking beer and bullshitting. After one too many drinks, J.J. toppled the bucket of bait onto the pier with his foot. Too intoxicated to care, but mostly because they were the only two people out that day, they left the dying bait fish there for the birds to prey on. Within the hour, what liquid was left in the fish had dried up in the hot sun. Eventually the odor was so heavy J.J. and Tatter got up and left. It smelled like that—dead fish guts baking in the sun. Whatever it was, it was awful and was either close by or the wind was picking up enough to carry it a good distance.

Either way, it freaking reeked.

With the pistol still in one hand, he pinched his nose with the other. The effort was futile, the smell had already ingrained within the fibers of his nostril hairs. With one more look around at the scene, J.J. rounded the back side of Patty's van, turned off the headlights, retrieved the keys from the ignition, and shut the door.

When he turned to make his way back toward the patrol car, he felt the ground shake beneath his feet. He paused for a second, looked around, and holstered his firearm. Shaking his head, he took two more concerned steps forward. His boots sloshed with wet disdain and then it happened again. The earth shook and J.J. almost lost his balance. He stopped, looking around but saw nothing.

Okay, man... he said to himself. *Starting tomorrow we need to lay off the booze. If you can't even stand up straight, how do you plan on keeping your cool when you write up a report on all the shit you've seen tonight?*

With that thought came a new one; all the shit he had seen tonight.

J.J. swallowed hard and started to feel sick again.

He stood there a second longer waiting for the nausea to pass. Last thing he wanted was for Patty to see him lose his meal for the second time.

"Speaking of that…" he breathed. "She's probably been sitting in that car long enough to have smelled the beer by—"

J.J.'s muttered words were cut short by the rumbling force of the ground. This time it was bigger and he had to grab hold of Patty's van bumper to keep from falling. The smell was stronger now and this time he thought he heard something.

It was thunderous like the storm, but wasn't the storm at all. It was lower. Quieter even. More like heavy breathing magnified through a cone. It was dense and eerie.

The earth quaked again and he felt a sudden sharp pain lash out around his entire midsection. It was instant and intense, causing him to nearly black out. When he regained awareness, he was being plummeted through the air by whatever had hold of him.

Then he saw… *her*.

J.J. screamed as she lifted him higher and higher into the air.

The mammoth beast's head was jagged, her entire body made of what looked like the elements of the ocean surface. Stone and rock lined her body into its hideous and deformed shape. Her face was covered in eyes on top of eyes and with a mouth even more jagged than her body. In that single moment, J.J. couldn't say how he knew that it… this thing… was a she. Regardless, in the chaos of his mind processing the truth as it poured out around him like the vines of a poisonous plant, he could see the breasts. All of them. They covered her chest like some kind of deformed cat. The nipples protruded like serrated things ready for the succulent touch of her litter's lips.

The thing lifted him higher into the air, roaring with rage.

The air filled with its stench. Her taunting growl echoed out for all to hear.

Frantic, J.J.'s eyes darted left and right. There was nothing he could do. Nowhere to go. He was caught in her clutches, her grip too strong for him to even squeeze his arm in to retrieve his pistol. Overwhelmed with disbelief, the lines started to blur, and the young officer started to fade. Focus was no longer an option.

He screamed again, looking around, the fog of what was happening making him go numb all over... or was that her grip? He couldn't feel his body. His legs.

His eyes jumped around in hope of one last ounce of fight. There was nothing. All he could see were the cookie cutter homes down below. He had to be more than twenty stories up. He stole one last look at the creature and then back at the earth.

The last thing he saw before it all went black was the Dalmatian fire hydrant.

He saw it soaring toward him, getting closer and closer within milliseconds.

The last thought he had before slamming headlong into the gravel wasn't even a profound one.

Stupid hydrant, he thought, his skull splitting wide against the asphalt road.

His brains and face sprayed across the ground, the impact so great that his meaty chunks disintegrated into liquefied particles of red and pink mist.

With his limp body still in her grasp, she flung him to the ground again and again and again. Each time she did, what was left of his body became less and less. Turning meat and bone into a mash of seeping goo. The giant beast squeezed what was left in her palm.

There was nothing of J.J. left except color and liquid.

Not even his pistol.

Just when the Old One turned from the liquefied police officer toward his patrol car and the sardine trapped inside, the bodies of both Scotty and Ms. Hines started to squirm. Scotty's body convulsed, sending a spew of squid-like things onto the road. They slithered away into the night, set on finding hosts for the feast. Ms. Hines rose to her feet and sluggishly shambled off into the night.

Moments later, Scotty Watts did the same, staggering to his feet in a slow shuffle through the rain. His intestines and muck dripped from the open cavity that had once been his stomach. A bloody puddle of red and meaty chunks was left in his wake. Where he was headed didn't matter so long as the larva controlling his steps eventually found substance to quench the palate.

Patty screamed as the monster lifted the cruiser.

She tried the door but couldn't get out.

It didn't matter.

It was too late.

She was sailing through the air toward a phone pole just like that.

Her death wasn't instant, the crash only paralyzing her.

When the car and the debris settled, she tried to breathe but the pain was too great.

What ended it for Patty was when the giant she-thing stomped the car into the earth with anger.

Its roar of rage echoed out into the night.

For some, it would be mistaken as meaningless thunder.

However, for most of Topsail it meant the end.

ELEVEN

The Drake'o house was quiet.

The kids were dead asleep in the other room. Blake had put up a fuss about it, never having actually slept over before. The little boy had the nerve to tell Tatter that his house was creepy and smelled funny. Blake's claim to restlessness was that the place was haunted. For a minute, Tatter agreed with the kid, lingering on the thought that his wife still haunted him, waiting for him to meet her on the other side of life. Rather than spook the child any more than he already was, he ushered him back to sleep and assured him that there was nothing to worry about.

Truth was; there was plenty to worry about.

Patty had never been late picking up the kids from work. If she ever stayed late at the diner to get in a few extra hours, she had always called. Even still, she was always back in time to see the kids off to bed at her own house.

Worried about her, he skipped over the watered down beer in the garage refrigerator and made a glass of scotch on the rocks. It burned the back of his throat, just the way he liked it. With a few coughs and one or two smaller sips from his glass to chase the throat irritation away, Tatter was back in the living room.

The place seemed cold. Thoughts of The Old One being a reality gave him the chills.

The rain steadily fell outside, and at times, the wind got so rough he could hear it whistling through the trees in his front yard. The television was still on, the DVD menu for Shrek on repeat—the volume muted.

Wondering what the weather and Tropical Strom Faye was up to had him sitting on the couch and raising the volume just enough to hear without waking the kids. He changed the channel to the local weather and waited for the commercials to cycle through. *The Swiffer Wet Jet.*

The Mr. Clean Magic Eraser. And yes, some silly depression medication that had more side effects than watching Dr. Phil while on LSD. The one thing Tatter never understood about those stupid medicine commercials was the part about anal leakage. No one in their right mind would take a medication that resulted in anal leakage. That was just wrong on so many levels.

When the weather finally kicked on, he didn't realize it at first, but he wasn't even listening. His mind was elsewhere. Rather than pay attention to the Tropical Strom Faye updates, he found himself thinking about his wife and how he missed her. It was, at least in his opinion, very possible that she haunted the house waiting for him to die. Ever since she left, all he wanted to do was die. He just needed to be with her again. He didn't know what else do without her. If it weren't for his strange addiction to those stupid internet sites and J.J., he would have been a lost cause.

Which in turn got him thinking about Max.

He could only imagine what the man was going through. Hanna was dead and her death was fresh. Tatter thought about how devastated he had been when his wife had passed away. How hard it had been, not only on him, but the kids as well. It was like he had lost it all. In truth, he had. She was his everything. Tatter had seen Max and Hanna together. She was that man's everything, too. No doubt about it.

Tatter took a deep breath, chugged a burning gulp of scotch, and shook his head.

There were only three types of men in this world and they could all be measured by the weight of losing a loved one. Some people, like Tatter, reacted the way most people do. They curl up in the fetal position and wither away. It takes them months… sometimes even years, if at all, to come out of that lull and into the world again. Others lash out with rage, hurting themselves and loved ones. The lucky ones have a strong support group, and over time, if not taken by suicide, learn to adapt and calm down. Max, on the other hand, was neither of these. No, he was the third type of man. Honestly, that scared Tatter more. The third type of man seemed to just hold it all in. Treat it as if nothing had happened. Granted, Tatter hadn't been there when it happened, but that didn't matter. He had just spent the last hour in Max's presence, and if Hanna really was dead... murdered... he wasn't showing any real signs. Denial was like that. It falls heavy on the third type of man so thick it takes months before they come to grips with the fact that any of it had happened. Sure, right now that was great. It was helping Max keep his shit together. Helping the mechanic think with his head rather than his heart, but that was a dangerous thing. If and when the shit finally came full circle and hit him like a sack of fighting raccoons, the last thing anyone would want is to be there. That type of man... type three... was an explosion of carnage just waiting to happen. For some, it could happen in a day or two—generally at the funeral. Or worse, years down the road when they find themselves working a dead-end job they hate, lost in the house they had bought with their spouse. That would be when everyone was in trouble. All that postal nonsense you see on television—the guy that takes an M16 to work and cuts into everybody—that was the type three guy.

And Max was that man.

Tatter brought the glass of scotch to his lips. The ice bounced around inside, sliding across the glass to reach his lips. No juice. He was out. He looked down at the empty drink and sighed.

"Time for another," he said, jiggling the ice around inside the glass.

The ice clinked louder than he expected. He froze for a second, half expecting Blake to come walking down the hall with a frustrated yawn. The kid never came, and after a moment, the tall lanky fisherman stood up to make his way back to the garage for another drink.

As he paced across the house toward the garage the buzz started kicking in. That's what he liked about liquor. No bloated feeling. And no constant trips to the pisser. Just sip and feel good. Well, in his case, it was more like gulps, but who was keeping track of that kind of thing anyway?

With his glass replenished, he shuffled back down the hall toward the living room. He stopped for a second, tiptoeing toward the guest bedroom. He cracked the door open and stepped inside to take a peek. The door creaked and groaned. Tatter gritted his teeth as he eased into the room, hoping the sound wouldn't wake them.

It hadn't.

They were both out cold.

Blake snuggled tightly against his pillow and Peggy was sprawled out like a tarantula on the bed. All her limbs were stretched out as far as they could go. The only part of her body actually covered up with blankets was one elbow, her head not even on the pillow.

Tatter chuckled under his breath and eased back out of the room.

He started to close the door, but it groaned even louder than when he had opened it. So he left it cracked and eased back into the hallway. When he felt far enough away from the room, he went back to walking normal.

It felt weird having other people in the house at this time of night. Normally, by now, J.J. would have been on his way home and Tatter would have been left drinking scotch and surfing his silly Bizarro site. It felt good in a way, but in truth, all it did was make him realize how alone he had become.

After a few more sips of scotch, he eased up into his computer chair and stared at the screen. His mind felt like fuzz, the alcohol working steadily through his system.

The page that had been left up was a detailed explanation of those squids that had attacked Max's wife. Cephanisio was the name. He skimmed the page trying to remember the last thing he had read from it.

He just couldn't believe it. If the stories he had heard about the Old One as a child were real, no one was safe.

He skimmed the page again.

If it were a snake, it would have jumped out and bit him. A moment later, he found it, then started reading aloud to himself.

"A loose pantheon of ancient, powerful deities from space who once ruled the Earth and who have since fallen into a deathlike sleep were once feared by man. Forced into the deep by an ancient ritual found in the book of Necrodine, all but one remains." *The Necrodine*, Tatter thought. *Why does that sound so familiar?* He thought about it for a second but it never came to him. He read on. "She is known as the Old One. For centuries, she has been dormant at the ocean floor awaiting the day that fate would allow her to return to the surface and reclaim divinity over mankind."

Below this were half a dozen astrological symbols Tatter knew nothing about. Something about the alignment of some planets he had never heard of that were a part of a solar system he had never heard of.

Other than that, there were a few other links at the bottom of the page. Related links and suggested material.

When he browsed them, Tatter tensed.

The third one from the left read: Operation Bumblebee—The Ritual.

Tatter didn't waste any time. Sure enough, the link just took him to a different page on the same site. That was a good sign. A lot of the times those links were just decoys that would send you to porn sites or spam pop-ups that suggested you won a million bucks. He didn't have any time for that sort of thing. He was of an age that his dick would never see the straight side of a pencil ever again, and at his age, who cared about money? All that crap was just one big scam anyway.

Glad that it was an actual site link, he waited for the page to load.

He took two swigs of scotch and stared at the screen, watching the content slowly come together. The weather was obviously interfering with the internet connection. It always slowed down when it was raining for some reason. Now it was going slower than hell.

He gritted his teeth and found himself chugging the rest of the scotch as a result of the built up tension.

More waiting.

He tapped his fingers on the desk.

When the page finally finished loading, Tatter wasn't at all surprised at what he saw.

At the top of the new site page were a few photos. The top black and white photo was of the museum downtown. The title of the photo read in big block letters: *TOP SECRET RITUAL GROUNDS.*

In the photo below there were more than a dozen men and women dressed in traditional scientist attire. Beside them in the photo was a large round rock about five feet in height. They all stood in a row next to the rock wearing white overcoats. Most of them had thick bottle-cap glasses like the ones Tatter wore. Seeing all of them wearing the glasses made him subconsciously shift the glasses on his face.

He scrolled down further to read the caption under the photo of the scientists. It read: *The book on Necrodine helped develop many of the modern day advances in science. Things like Solar energy and Star mapping would be nonexistent without its discovery.*

Tatter took another glance at the second black and white photo. Sure enough… there it was. The book. The second scientist to the left held out a strange looking leather bound book. It looked old and mysterious, and it seemed out of place in the shiny bright photo.

He stared at the photo for a moment longer and then recognized someone… *Holy shit*! He recognized B—

A loud thunderous *boom* rocketed through the house like falling timber. But it was metallic in nature. Like a car crash, only amplified.

Tatter jumped.

Someone screamed—the children.

Then everything went black.

The power was out.

"Son of a…" Tatter muttered, pushing out of his computer chair. He made his way through the dark and into the kitchen. He could hear the kids calling out from down the hall.

"It's okay, kids…" Tatter replied loudly, but with a comforting tone. "We just lost power is all. That kind of thing happens all the time with storms like this."

He fumbled blindly through the cabinets for a flashlight.

Fishing one out, he turned it on and faced it toward the hall.

Two bright shiny faces flashed back at him, their bulging eyes startling him so bad he almost jumped right out of his overalls.

Blake and Peggy stood before him, eyes wide and filled with fear.

"What was that?" Blake cried, wiping sleep from his eyes.

"It was just…"

Peggy reached up and grabbed his pants leg. "I'm scared."

"No need to be scared, kids." Tatter knelt down to meet them eye to eye. "It was probably just that old rotted oak tree beside the house that finally decided to come down with the wind blowing so hard. I'll go check it out in a minute. Why don't you two make it back to bed?"

"But I can't sleep," Blake hissed.

"I want my mommy," Peggy pleaded.

"I know, baby." Tatter sighed, hugging both of them. "Your mom is on her way. I promise."

Tatter felt something swell in his throat. Somehow that promise just felt like one big fat lie.

Just when he was about to suggest the kids make their way into the living room while he got some candles together, the loud rattling boom hit again.

This time it was closer and no longer metallic.

The house shook.

Peggy screamed.

Then the sour salty stench came. It filled the house instantly. It was awful.

TWELVE

George Braidy tapped on the window. "Would you look at that?" His left cheek bulged with tobacco.

Tatter's crap-car rolled to a sputtering stop and Max's eyes went wide as he gripped the steering wheel tightly.

They had both spent the better part of the drive in silence. George suggested that it would help Max focus on the road. Seeing how stressed the tubby old man was, Max didn't argue. George was right. The weather was rough, making it hard to see. In the silence, the rain beating down on the hood like massive metal pellets, time seemed to crawl. He wasn't sure if the clock on the dash was accurate or not, but regardless, it was getting late. It felt late. If the time on Tatter's car was right then it had good reason to feel that way. They had been driving for more than fifteen minutes and had only made it halfway through Topsail. If things didn't clear up soon it would be another fifteen minutes before they got to the diner and the police station, putting their arrival time right at 1am.

Max couldn't think of the last time he had stayed up this late. Working as a mechanic for so long, he had become accustomed to rising before the sun.

His eyes stung with tiredness.

So far, all they had seen was the same old thing. Rain. Wind. Fallen trees and debris littering the road from the storm.

About five, maybe ten minutes back, they witnessed the blackout. Power went out all over town. What few lights were on in various homes along Main Street blinked out at the exact moment the streetlights shut off. Surprisingly, without the lights pressing a dense smog of reflective mist, it was actually easier to see. Max was thankful for that, plain and simple. Had the street lights still been on, the glare might have made him drive headlong into the fallen tree that they were parked in front of now. Luckily, he saw it in time and Tatter's brakes held. It blew Max's mind that they did, considering. After he and George shook off the near fatal collision with the fallen tree, they determined they needed to find an alternate route. Best way would be to cut over to the next block and go around.

The car sputtered violently to a near gurgling sound as Max backed up and got them turned around. They had to backtrack a block to make the turn. Once they did, they were on 13th street riding with the beach on their right.

The moment they had rounded the corner onto 13th Street was when George tapped on the window.

There was just no way that all this was happening.

If the fallen tree and weathered debris on Main Street was devastating, then this was hell… literal hell had come to visit Topsail, and it was bleeding forth from the sea.

The slithering leech-like squids covered the street. They poured in from the beach. The road looked as if it was pulsing with movement. They were working their way through the road and deeper into town, slinking through the yards and homes off to Max's left.

"Where the hell do you think they're all going?" Max asked.

"Who gives a flying fuck, Max?" George demanded. "Let's get the hell out a here before they start crowding the car."

That was when Max realized that they were in fact gravitating toward the car.

Like one solid color of gray, slimy glistening muck, they surged forward.

"Move!" George shouted.

Then the first one lunged into the air and *slapped* hard against the windshield. Max flinched as it collided with the glass. Just before it had smacked against the thick glass, he could visibly make out the sharp, hideous teeth. Its tentacles lashed out, trying to grab hold, but it was no use. The creature slid down the window along with the falling rain.

Max tensed and slammed his foot down on the gas pedal. The car choked and staggered forward. The engine roared with a high pitched squeal, but didn't accelerate much at all.

"Drive!" George yelled over the whining engine just as two dozen of those things leaped into the air toward the car.

"I'm trying!" Max demanded, shaking the steering wheel with begging suggestiveness.

Five or six of the slimy things plummeted into the windshield, all unable to grab hold of the slick surface.

Another one hit hard and the window cracked.

"Come on!" Max cried, pumping the pedal.

The car inched forward.

Three more squid hit the window and then the car took off. The high pitched whine of the engine equalized, coming back down to a normal tone. The tires caught traction and the vehicle shot forward in a flash. Max's neck rocketed backward as his shoulders collided with the seat. He heard George choke on his tobacco and start cursing while he spat, but he didn't have time to look. The car rolled over the slimy creatures as it plowed through them.

As the car picked up speed, reaching 45 miles an hour, the squid they passed by that didn't get trampled in the wake of the car tires, lunged out, attacking the car from all sides. They collided with the metal frame at the same consistency as the falling rain. The squishing *splat* the creatures made as they were crushed by the spinning tires reminded Max of stomping them out in his living room. That little *yelp* they made with each one he killed. Only now, that sound was magnified and didn't seem to end. It was just one long drawn out high pitched cry as the car moved forward running over more and more of them with each inch forward.

Max tried to shake the thought from his mind and focus on the road. The car started to slide to the right, the tires not keeping traction with all the slimy goo and rain on the road.

Focus... Focus, he thought. *Don't need to lose it. Not right now.*

Adjusting his steering, the car kept straight.

When he looked up, glancing in the rearview mirror for only a split second, Max saw something he wished wasn't true.

There were squids jumping into house windows all up and down the block. The only thing was, the windows weren't nearly as thick as the car windshield. He watched as one leaped up, shattering the house window as if it was thin ice.

They were breaking into the houses.

Max saw his chance and took it. The block ended and he took an immediate left which would put him back on Main Street.

It wasn't until he took the turn that he realized how fast he was going. The car leaned hard on the passenger side and Max thought he heard George cringe. In his peripheral vision, he saw the chubby old man brace for impact.

Max gripped the wheel so tightly that his knuckles went white. The car leveled out and he eased off the gas.

He took a right on Main Street and locked eyes with George. The blank, pale expression of horror and disbelief plastered across his neighbor's face matched his own.

As the car kept moving down the road toward the station, only one thought kept repeating in Max's mind.

When George finally spoke up, it was a confirmation that they were both on the same page.

George's voice was soft and distant. "They're getting into the houses..." He stared off into the darkness, and when he spoke again, Max almost couldn't even hear him. "All those people sleeping..."

THIRTEEN

Amanda Potts was jarred from a deep sleep when something outside her room crashed loud and hard to the floor. It sounded like it had happened in the den. Maybe the kitchen.

The shattering of glass, perhaps.

She wasn't sure.

The haze of deep sleep rolled over her as she sat up in bed, slightly startled.

The memory of what she had been dreaming wrestled against reality as she realized she was sitting up in bed.

The dream had been a good one, too. She had just won the lottery and managed to do so without anyone knowing about it. With the billions sitting snug in her offshore bank account, she was set. No more working at the daycare, dealing with those spoiled little brats. No more coming home tired and sickly from all the germs those little tyrants carried around with them. No more changing diapers on a toddler that didn't even belong to her. Someone else could shovel their shit for a change. That's all daycare had been to her. A hell where parents got to drop of their devil-spawn because they were tired of dealing with it. Well, they couldn't pawn them off on her any more, because she was rich. In her dream, she had just made it to work and was getting scolded by her boss for showing up late. With a big finger pointed in her face and her boss's temper flared, Amanda smiled. This was her chance to tell him to fuck off. Tell them all to piss off and shove it. Her boss finally quit griping and the words were just about to roll off her tongue when the sudden sound pulled her from her dream.

You can take this job and shove it... I'm moving to Italy! She thought, rubbing her eyes as she sat there in bed.

She had worked that stupid job for the last three years and hated every minute of it. Only reason she had even lasted this long at the stupid place was because there just weren't that many jobs on the island. And she wasn't one for having a long commute to work.

Something stirred in the kitchen, reminding her of the noise that had pulled her from the bliss of slumber.

"Shelly…" She whispered, looking down at her girlfriend of more than two years. "Did you hear that? Someone is in the house."

Shelly didn't move.

She was dead to the world.

Amanda envied that about her. She could sleep through just about anything.

"Shelly…" Amanda insisted, shaking her significant other.

Shelly shifted, rolling over with a groan of protest.

"Shelly, wake up." Amanda tried again, shaking her lover hard on the shoulder. "This is serious. I hear something."

"Then go check it out," Shelly spat, covering her head with the pillow.

Amanda and Shelly first met at the daycare. Yes, they both worked there… which in all honesty was one of the only real perks about the place. To most of the people who lived in Topsail, they were just roommates who happened to work the same job. They had hit it off from the start. To be honest about it, this was Amanda's first actual relationship with someone of the same sex. For Shelly, it was a different story. Everyone in Topsail knew that she was a lesbian. Amanda, on the other hand, you would have never guessed, and that was how she had hoped to keep it. Everyone thinking they were just roommates was fine with her.

She loved Shelly. That was true. But there were times when she still longed for the macho security that she found in dating guys.

Like right now for example.

Girlfriend hears spooky happenings in the other room in the middle of the night. A redneck boyfriend would get out of bed and appease her with a baseball bat or gun in hand while they checked things out. Shelly wasn't like that. Shelly was the girl in the relationship. Which left Amanda doing all the guy work. Squishing bugs, opening the car door, and yes… checking out the spooky noises in the middle of the night.

"Fine!" Amanda grumbled. "If I die or get raped, it's your fault."

When Amanda looked down, expecting a reply, Shelly was already sound asleep. A faint snore rustled under the pillow as she exhaled a long drawn out breath.

Amanda rolled her eyes and climbed out of bed.

The wood floor felt cold against her bare feet.

In the movies she had always seen the person going to check things out grab a weapon from beside the bed. When she looked to her left, the only thing leaning against the wall was an umbrella. She shrugged and took it into her hands. Her thoughts raced with infinite possibilities as she eased toward the bedroom door. A burglar was the first thing that came to mind. Then a big fat rat scavenging through the pantry. Her skin crawled at that image.

She reached out, grabbed the door handle, and looked back at Shelly.

She was out cold—oblivious to everything. Her snoring echoed across the silence and Amanda started shaking.

"Get a grip," she told herself. "Probably just some kids playing a prank."

The words made her feel better as she turned the knob and stepped out into the hallway. The prospect of it just being a prank was very likely. Over the last few weeks, one of her neighbors had been complaining that some of the local kids had been tearing up their garbage at night and making a lot of noise.

She hoped that was all this was as she found herself tip-toeing down the hall in nothing but a tight wife-beater and her panties—the umbrella probably not all that intimidating.

She laughed under her breath at how silly she felt and most likely looked.

The laugher quickly faded when she heard the noise again.

A loud *thump*.

It sounded dense and wet, like slapping a wet mop against a tile floor.

Amanda felt her chest tighten. It was then that she realized she had been holding her breath. She stopped halfway down the hall and just listened.

The sound happened again. This time she was certain it came from the kitchen.

What the hell is that? She breathed, lifting the umbrella up at the ready as if she knew what she planned to do with it.

The sound came again. It was so loud, Amanda jumped, nearly dropping the feeble weapon in her hands.

She took one more step forward and then froze. Her heart raced. She didn't like this one bit.

"Who's… who's there?" her voice quivered.

No one replied.

As she stood there in the silence, the distance between her and the kitchen seemed like miles. In truth, it was only about three more steps further into the hallway and then she should be there… able to investigate the strange noise. She didn't want to. Part of her just wanted to crawl back in bed, snuggle up against Shelly, and pretend she hadn't heard anything. The other part of her, the part edging her forward, knew better. She needed to see what was going on. If someone was stealing something, they needed to take whatever the hell it was they wanted and leave.

"I said, who's there?" She raised her voice, ready to start swinging wildly with the umbrella.

Another thump echoed out in the kitchen followed by some strange slithering sounds.

She swallowed hard, her nerves getting the best of her. Her throat protested as what felt like rocks started snaking down into her stomach. Her palms began to sweat as she gripped the umbrella tighter.

She gritted her teeth and cursed the fact that Shelly wasn't behind her right now, protecting her.

"Fuck it…" she muttered under her breath, and then took two wide berthing steps into the kitchen from the hallway.

At first, she didn't see anything. There was no one there.

Relief fell over her like the Holy Spirit at a Sunday service. She almost started to raise her hands in thankfulness, but stopped in mid-stride.

The sound.

The slithering wet sound.

The thought of soapy water squishing between your fingers came to mind. Amanda wasn't frightened. No, not at first. The emotion that consumed her at first was one of bewilderment and a sense of disconnectedness. What she was seeing didn't make any sense. Not unless the neighborhood punks had decided to play a damn prank on her house.

But squid? She thought. *Why would kids throw squid through my kitchen window? They're still alive?*

Amanda stared at her kitchen floor with disgust. There had to be half a dozen of them sliding across the cold tile. The gray goo that followed in their wake as they slid across the floor was disgusting. It smelled disgusting. It was… wrong.

"What the fuck?" she grunted, craning her neck toward the broken kitchen window. There were two more of those gross things creeping, crawling across her sink onto the kitchen counter. "Those stupid kids are gonna fuckin' pay. I can't believe thi—"

Amanda's sentence was cut short when one the squids leaped from the floor in front of her. Startled at the sight, she screamed as the thing cleared more than four feet into the air. In a panic, she took a step back and swung the umbrella with her right hand. The tip of the makeshift weapon crashed into the dishwasher and she lost hold of it. The rustling *smack* the umbrella made as it collided with the tile floor sent all of the squirming things into the air.

"Ahh…" Amanda shouted, staggering backward into the hall. She shouted for Shelly to come to her aid as she fell on her ass on the hallway floor. "Shelly… help!"

It was no use. The creatures were on her instantly. When Amanda looked over her shoulder back toward the open door that led into the bedroom, Shelly did not come. No, that stupid bitch could sleep through just about anything. Even the screams of death.

Amanda flinched as she felt sharp pain on her hand. When she looked down, one of the slimy gray things was taking a chunk from her knuckles—its tentacles wrapped tightly around her wrist. She started to scream again, but the sharp stabbing sensation that burned at her throat was too much. All that came from her lips was a gagging protest of pain.

The creature dug through the skin of her throat with ease, its razor sharp teeth slicing through her skin in seconds. It wiggled with excitement as it burrowed into her from the outside.

Amanda gagged, feeling it tear through her. Feeling the blood splash out from under her neck all over her chest and shoulders. The blood felt warm and soothing against her cold skin. Yet terrifying and horrid. This just couldn't be happening. There was no way. Then the thing inside of her dug deeper. She could feel it. She could feel all of them. Biting her hands and arms. Biting her left knee and her feet. Lying there on her back while they did all of this, her eyes remained wide open. Somehow the pain fizzled to a dulling numbness. Her mind clouded with comprehension. She was dying. The thing in her stomach twitched, making her feel sick. As life for Amanda faded and the darkness consumed her soul, her eyes remained on the hallway ceiling. The last human thought that pulsed through her brain was a simple question.

Why do all ceilings have ruffles and bumps? Why can't they be smooth like the walls?

What finally killed Amanda wasn't those things eating at her meaty flesh, or the thing digging deep into her belly to lay eggs. No, it was the blood that had piled in her throat and mouth forcing her lungs to fill with that same red, irony substance.

Amanda choked to death.

Only, that wasn't her last thought. It was mere moments later that her body trembled with new life. Abomination in death. An existence she could not at all comprehend.

When her eyes refocused, she was looking at the ceiling again. Only this time something felt different. It was as if she were in a tunnel of some kind, far back in the depths of her mind. She willed herself to scream. Call out for Shelly to come to her aid. But she couldn't. Instead all that surfaced was a gurgling moan. Yet, it hadn't been her that made the noise. It had been something in her. As much was also true when she found herself staggering to her feet. No matter how much she willed herself to do anything, it was as if something else had control. She tried to move forward toward the phone in the kitchen, but her body wouldn't let her. That *thing* inside her wouldn't let her. Paralyzed with fear and the reality of what was happening swept over Amanda like a horrendous nightmare. No longer in control of her own body, she watched consciously as the thing inside her pulled her to her feet. She watched as it forced her to turn and walk back into the bedroom where Shelly was still fast asleep. Something caught her peripheral and the thing inside forced her to look. The closet mirror in the bedroom reflected a grotesque sight.

Amanda was dead… and consciously she knew it. She could feel the thing inside forcing her forward, toward Shelly on the bed. The reflection of herself that she had momentarily seen in the mirror was horrifying. Her wife-beater sleep shirt was covered in blood. The cavity in her throat was still pulsing anew with red blood. Her skin was pale and her eyes were sunken back with dark circles around them. She looked… dead. She felt dead.

If the worst part of the nightmare wasn't realizing that after death she was somehow up and being forced forward by the thing inside of her, it was watching what happened next. With her eyes wide, all she could do was take in the new information. She screamed inside her head, trying like hell to wake Shelly, but it was no use. Again, the only noise that left her lips were muffled gurgling grunts.

Suddenly a new emotion surged through her. One she had never felt before. Hunger on a primordial level. The thing, the sluggish thing inside of her needed to feed. It needed her to feed for it. On the inside, Amanda cried as she watched herself climb into the bed and over Shelly. Internally, she cried at what she knew was coming next. She screamed with horror while she watched herself lean in and take that first bite.

Amanda's mouth wrapped tight around Shelly's jugular, her teeth sinking in deep. The warm taste of iron filled her mouth as flesh tore from her girlfriend's throat.

Shelly awoke in a fit of pain and shock. She grabbed at her wound, blood pooling violently around her onto the sheets and pillows.

Amanda cried, wanting to wake up. Wanting for all of this to end. This nightmare was just too much.

Only, it didn't end, and no matter how hard she tried, she wasn't waking up. Somehow in the deepest parts of her soul she knew that this was real. She knew what had happened in the kitchen was real. She had died and she could feel it. Even now, the rotting and decomposition that was taking place. Her mind raced with panic as the thing inside her forced her to feed on Shelly.

Shelly was dead. She wasn't moving. Her eyes were wide and soullessly vacant. And yet, Amanda couldn't stop, no matter how much she willed it. She just kept eating. Everything was red and wet with chunks of white and pink. She could feel the thick meat as it went down inside of her to that... thing.

Amanda sobbed, unable to bear it anymore, but it didn't matter, because she wasn't in control.

All she could do was watch. Her consciousness was all that she had left of herself.

Eventually, when there was nothing recognizably left of her dead girlfriend's face, the thing inside of Amanda forced her out of bed and to her feet. She quivered with fear, wondering where it was taking her. What it was going to do next. As she turned, leaving the bed, she saw two of those things slither past her toward Shelly. She was unable to look back to see what was happening, because the thing inside forced her forward into the hallway. For some reason, she felt like she knew. They were getting inside of Shelly just like they had done to her. These were not squid... these were something else. Something demonic.

As she shuffled down the hall toward the living room, Amanda could hear things happening in the bedroom. It sounded like Shelly was getting up and moving around. But that was impossible. She was dead. Amanda's soul groaned with dispute, but it was no use.

Against her will, the thing inside forced her into the living room. Just as she thought it was going toward the door, it veered hard left and charged forward toward the living room window.

Amanda Potts was in the air and through the window before she realized it. The sound of glass shattered around her as she felt the jagged shards cut at her face, shoulders, arms and legs. When the thing inside forced her to stand again, she found herself in the front yard. The wind and rain beat down like pelting needles of violence. Her body and eyes seemed to scan the area around her.

What Amanda saw was the most frightening thing of all.

The entire block was littered with people, all of whom looked like they had recently jumped through their own windows. Covered in cuts. Covered in blood. As the thing inside forced her forward, she got a good look at the block and realized there had to have been more than thirty people standing out in the street with her.

Every last one of them had that same blank lifeless stare.

Something crashed behind her.

Her body rocketed around to investigate so fast she almost toppled over. It was Shelly… she was climbing through the broken living room window. Her face was maimed from what had been done in the bedroom. If the window had cut her any, Amanda couldn't tell.

Then Shelly shuffled to her feet. The thing inside Amanda was no longer interested in Shelly. It forced her to turn around and start walking.

The last thing Amanda saw of her girlfriend was her eyes. That same blank stare. For a brief moment, she could tell… Shelly was conscious inside of it all, just like her. Just like all of them.

Amanda Potts snapped.

Her brain couldn't take it.

Like a twig, it just gave under the pressure.

Amanda screamed and didn't stop screaming for the rest of the night. Only, the screams were all just in her conscious mind.

The thing that was her body seemed to pay no attention and just kept walking and walking.

They all walked.

FOURTEEN

Business had long since closed by the time Max and George finally pulled into the diner's parking lot. The place was normally packed at this time of night, but with the storm stirring things up like it had been, the 24 hour eatery was as vacant as a roach infested Motel 6 on a Tuesday night. At one time, the diner had actually been a Waffle House. It was the same as all the rest—narrow and cramped. However, one of the locals had bought the building when the Waffle House closed down. The tall yellow block sign with black letters that read 'Waffle House' still stood, but were never turned on. Other than that the only thing different about the building was the owner had decided to paint it blue top to bottom, both inside and out. The place was never even given a name. Most of the locals just called it 'the diner.' Max and Hanna had asked a few people why it was never renamed, but no one ever seemed to have an answer. In truth, the town was probably small enough that giving the place a name didn't really matter. All that mattered was that they were open all night and always had a fresh pot of coffee brewing. Despite the fact that the place was pretty run down and probably wouldn't pass a health inspection, it was a damn good place to eat and had the best burgers in town. It was located just a few miles east of the Surf City Bridge and was about three blocks inland from the beach. And Max didn't even want to think about that. The sooner they got away from the water, the better. He knew good and well that George felt the same way about it. Neither one of them had to speak up on that one. The tension in the car was so thick, after what they had seen on 13th street, they just locked eyes and knew what the other was thinking. It was time to get the hell out of Dodge. Even still, they made a promise to Tatter and needed to get to the station. Someone had to be warned of what was happening. If anyone would believe them, that is.

"The lights ain't on inside," George noted, staring at the building through the rain.

Max squinted to get a better look past the rain beating down on the windshield. "The power's out all up and down Topsail, remember?" He shook his head, blurring the condensation on the wipe window with his sleeve. "But I can see a light on in there."

"What are you talkin' 'bout, boy?" George said. "I don't see nothin'."

"Looks like someone has some candles burning inside."

"Well, that don't mean they're open. And besides... I don't see Patty's car anywhere. She must have left already. We should use your cell to call him and see if she made it."

"I would..." Max shrugged, his eyes still fixed on the faint light coming from inside the diner. "But the land lines are down. Tatter's house phone didn't work when we left his place."

"Shit... You're right."

"Either way," Max nodded, pointing toward the diner. "Someone's in there. Even if it isn't Peggy and Blake's mom, we need to warn them. Tell them to go home or leave town. Those things are going to be coming inland and they don't have much time. You saw how many of them there w—"

"That's exactly why we don't need to be goin' in there." George pointed out the window, cutting Max short. "We ain't got no time for that, either. There were hundreds of those fuckin' slime buckets comin' up from the beach. Patty ain't here. We know that for sure. And she is the only reason we came here. So let's go before we get swarmed by the damn things."

"But..."

"But nothin', Max," George protested, spitting tobacco to the floorboard of Tatter's car and wiped his lip. "Patty ain't in there. Now let's get away before the shit hits the fan."

"I do believe the fan has already been more than reamed with crap at this point," Max argued. The smell of George's tobacco juice wafted in the air filling the rusted out car with its minty aroma. "What if it were Hanna in there, George?"

"But it ain't her. Hanna is dea—" It was no use. Max climbed out of the car and slammed the door shut. He was jogging through the rain toward the diner with his head low before George could finishing what he was saying. "Shit…" The large man gritted his teeth. "You're gonna end up gettin' us killed, kid."

George sat there watching the young auto mechanic race across the parking lot toward the door. The rain came down hard and everything beyond the parking lot was obscure as hell outside without any of the street lights on to illuminate the darkness. He sat for a second longer and heard the bell on the diner door chime as Max went inside. It was quiet. Too quiet. He didn't like any of this one bit. With those things on the loose and what was happening to the people of Topsail, he had the right mind to head back to the house and get his guns just before hitting the Surf City bridge and getting the hell out of town. Fuck going to the police station to report any of this. Either the cops already knew about it or would think it was all some kind of prank. They couldn't afford that kind of time. Hell, they couldn't afford this kind of time, either. Max was being reckless. Not thinking straight. Maybe Hanna's death was starting to get to him.

A sudden brushing sound reverberated in the darkness somewhere off to George's left. When he looked, he didn't see anything. Tension gripped at his heart like a vice. Sweat formed on his forehead. Or was that just the fact that he was soaking wet from the rain? He couldn't tell. He wiped his forehead with his sleeve, looked down at the key in the ignition and the dangling keychain photo of Tatter holding up a small bass. The lanky old man had a creepy smile. George felt the silence around him growing thicker. He didn't like that. He swallowed hard, snatched the keys from the ignition, and climbed out of the car.

"I can't believe that prick just left me out here alone," he breathed, bouncing heavily across the parking lot. The rain beat down around him soaking deeper into his already drenched attire. "That's just unacceptable."

He felt his sides burn as he jogged across the small parking lot toward the front door. It ached like a sharp stabbing sensation. If they were caught in an on foot situation he knew he was going to be screwed. He was out of shape. No doubt about it. But he didn't want to think about it. By the time he reached the diner door and swung it open, his breathing had become heavy and shallow. The bell chimed as he entered. The *ding... ding... ding...* was so loud in the silence that to him it sounded more like an advertising alert that echoed through the storm. If there was anyone or anything beyond what his eyes could see in the streets, then they sure as hell knew he had just went through that door.

When the door slammed shut, George swirled around and glared out into the parking lot. Everything was silent and still. He didn't like that at all. A flash of what had happened back at Max's house played out in his mind. Only this time, it was him getting killed and shot at here at the diner rather than that cop and those paramedics in the front yard. His chest contracted and a sharp pain surged through his torso like a jolt of lighting. He heaved a heavy gasp of air and clutched his chest with his right hand.

"You okay?" Max asked, stepping up behind him.

In truth, that was probably the dumbest question the old man had heard all night long. Of course, he wasn't okay. His best friend's wife was murdered. The cops and paramedics that showed up to take care of it were killed to turn around and become some kid of fucked up zombie. J.J. was drunk and driving out in this shit storm. And the power was out all across town. Now, here he was standing in the dark empty diner all on some hunch that someone was inside because of some flickering light.

George took another deep breath and calmed. "Yeah, I'll be fine. Just too much activity for an old man like me. I think it's 'bout time to go home and call it a day."

"Yeah…" Max agreed with a half forced smile. "That ain't no shit."

George grinned at the use of his own catch phrase and looked past Max.

The diner was empty. However, there was one single candle flickering in the center of the room atop the bar. The shadows in the room danced around with the small moving flame.

"See anything?" George whispered, his eyes focused on the flickering candle.

"Nothing," Max whispered back. "Nothing behind the counter and no one that I could tell in the back on the other side of the kitchen."

"Well, someone had to have lit the candle," George said. "Maybe they just forgot to blow it out when they left."

"True..." Max agreed, scratching at his thick black mustache. "But for it being an all-night diner where is everybody? Somebody still has to be here?"

"Maybe they all went home when the power went out?" George reasoned, stepping away from the door and further into the diner. He didn't like the eerie feeling he had been getting as a result of being so close to the door. At any moment, something from outside could come in and get him. He rubbed at his sore chest, and said, "Called it a day. Told everyone to go home for the night. No point in being here if the coffee ain't stayin' warm."

Max laughed and smiled. Again, it seemed overly forced and slightly terrified.

George tried to return the gesture but failed. It only came out as a dead glare of uncomfortable distain. He didn't like any of this and he could tell that Max knew it.

"You're right…" Max agreed. "It's possible that everyone already went home. I just wish I could call Tatter and see if Patty made it over there to pick up the kids. I'm worried about them being over there alone."

"You and me both," George said. "But right now, I am more worried about the two of us. We shouldn't be here. Not now. Let's get back to my place. Get some real weapons and cross the bridge into the mainland before we wish we had."

"But…"

"But, nothin'," George insisted. "Look… those things out there really are connected to the Old One. I know this because—"

A loud *thump* reverberated off the walls and George jumped.

Max jumped in response as well, and said, "What the hell was that?"

"I don't know," George whispered, pointing toward the bathrooms.

They both locked eyes for a few moments. The silence dug into their surroundings like thick sheets of air.

"We need to check it out," Max breathed.

"Like hell we do," George said, pulling on Max's shirt.

However, it was too late. The young mechanic was already turned away from George and easing himself down the narrow row of booths toward the bathrooms.

"This kind a shit's gonna get us killed," George hissed, shaking his head.

"Good." Max nodded, not turning to look at George. With his back turned, he just kept on toward the bathrooms. "At least I have my chance of seeing Hanna again."

"Fuck…" George breathed.

The old man looked around the room as he watched his friend slowly easing toward the restrooms. What little he could see of the parking lot from inside the diner was void of activity. He felt eased by this, but not by much. If those things on 13th street were making their way through town, it wouldn't be long before they made it here. The rain was still coming down hard and what trees lined the parking lot was blowing violently from side to side. The wind was kicking pretty hard. Surely, the storm would be over soon, but from the looks of it, he knew better than to think that. Even still, he could hope.

When he looked back up, he suddenly realized he had been standing still. Max was more than ten feet ahead of him, with a hand on the bathroom door and his ear pressed against it.

"I hear something," Max whispered, his ear still pressed against the men's restroom door.

"I don't hear anything," George replied. *But I do see something. You are not thinking with your head.* "Let's get out a here, Max. We need to go. We aren't safe here."

Before Max could argue any further, the loud *thump* came again.

The bathroom door shook.

"Oh, shit." Max back stepped.

George raised his shaking hand, wishing like hell that he had a gun at ready. He felt helpless and downright ignorant standing there empty handed. He needed something, anything to defend with.

That was when the bathroom door swung open and a woman screamed.

Jenny Kinley shrieked as she stepped back, obviously startled to see Max standing right there in front of her. She was topless, wearing only a pair of tight jeans, and a pair of bright orange shoes. Her large breasts bobbed up and down as she jumped, covering them with the black shirt that she had been in the process of putting back on. She was in her early twenties and worked nights at the diner. Her hair was long and blonde. She had a little meat to her but was nowhere near what anyone would call chunky. If you were a guy in Topsail, there was no question about it—you wished you could get into her pants, married or not. She was hot. In the bathroom behind her, Keith Boyed stood, pulling his pants to his waist. He didn't work at the diner, but might as well have with how much he hung around the place keeping Jenny company when things were slow. From the looks of it, he was doing a damn fine job of it, too. Keith was close to the same age as Jenny. They had both gone to school together. Although it was an unspoken thing, everyone in Topsail knew that they were destined to get married and live a long life on the island. If you asked either of them, they would have disagreed. Not about the being together part mind you. No, about the part where they would live in Topsail for the rest of their lives. Like all young people their age when the time presented itself for them to leave they planned on it. Where they were going to go or what they were going to do with their lives was one of the main gossip topics for most of the older ladies in Topsail. Max knew this all too well, because after about a year of living on the island, Hanna had been integrated into the gossip circles.

"Hey, what the fuck?" Keith demanded, wiping the sweat from his forehead while pulling his pants button together.

"Hey, Keith," Max said. "Sorry… we didn't mean to startle you, Jenny."

"Uhh…" Jenny gritted her teeth with disgust. She turned toward Keith and shoved him with her free hand, the other still covering her sizable breasts. "I thought you said you locked the front door?"

"I did…" Keith smiled, looking past her at Max and George.

Both men smiled back, and from the expression returned by the young man, he seemed to know that Max and George were jealous.

"Can't you guys see that the diner is closed?" Keith asked, his chest puffed up with pride.

"Get out…" Jenny hissed, shoving Keith out of the bathroom.

Keith chuckled as she shoved him out, closing the door behind him.

"Haa…" Keith smoothed his curly hair with one hand and rubbed his bare chest with the other. "Women."

"Sorry to interrupt, Keith," Max said. "But we came to check on Patty. She never showed up at Tatter's to pick up the kids."

"She left, dude." Keith smiled. "Everybody left a while ago. Power outage and all that."

"Right…" Max nodded. "That makes sense. But we saw the candle burning inside the diner, so we came in to see what was going on."

"Well…" George said. "By the looks of it, I'd say we found out."

"That, you did," Jenny said, stepping out of the bathroom with all her clothes on. "Please don't tell anybody, okay? I could get fired if anyone found out."

"Don't worry," George said. "We won't tell anyone."

"If there's anyone to tell come this time tomorrow." Max frowned.

"What do you mean?" Jenny's left brow lifted.

George stared at her for a moment while she pulled her long blonde hair back into a ponytail, then bod, "Nothing… he doesn't mean anything."

"Bullshit," Max barked. "Hanna is dead. Lots of people are *dead*!"

"What?" Both Jenny and Keith said together.

The diner fell silent. When George's eyes drifted over to the candle still flickering on the counter, he noticed the two half eaten pies, half a dozen roses, and the little black box. The kind of box that would hold a ring. That was when he noticed the shining stone flickering against what little light existed. It was on Jenny's left hand. He and Max had intruded on something more than just a little after hours activities. His chest tightened against the thought and took a deep breath to force the pain away. When George finally spoke up, he wished it was all a lie. That none of it was true. That it could all be taken back. But it couldn't. His grandfather had been right. Max had the right to know the truth. They all did.

"He's telling the truth." George's gaze dropped to the floor. "Hanna is dead. And if we stay here much longer, we will be too."

FIFTEEN

The Old diner parking lot was still silent.

After having intruded on the awkwardly special moment between Keith and Jenny, Max picked up on George's odd behavior. The large old man knew something and wasn't telling. Max's mind flashed back to that moment in Tatter's car right before nearly crashing headlong into the fallen tree in the middle of the road. George had been about ready to spill something... but what?

Keith was fully dressed now.

So was Jenny.

The candle on the counter still flickered, casting long dancing shadows across the floor and the kitchen.

George sat slouched on the bar on the first of five stools, seated all the way to the left. In front of him was the register. He stared absently at it with his head slouched to his chin.

The large man took a deep breath and sighed.

Having let it all out--telling Keith and Jenny what had transpired thus far. Telling them of the murders. The fight in Max's yard. Those things on 13th street that were more than likely headed this way.

They all sat in silence for a moment, the wind and rain outside loud and impending to their ears.

Even against the pale light, Max could see that it had taken a toll on George to tell what he had told. He looked tired, and for a moment, perhaps almost twice his age.

"No way that any of that shit is true, man." Keith stiffened his poster. The young man was standing next to George. He turned to Jenny and Max who were both seated behind him at one of the booths. "Come on... this is some kind of a joke, right?"

It took Max a moment to speak, but when he did he voice was stern and soft.

"I'm afraid so, Keith," Max stretched his arms out across the booth table, his eyes not once leaving Keith's. "Hanna is dead. And what George is telling you, all of it, is really. We aren't safe here."

"Oh my god," Jenny gasped under her breath.

She looked like she was about to start crying. Keith stepped toward her and stroked her hair.

"Well, if this shit is really real, there is no way somebody didn't know about it... right... *Right?"*

"Keep your voice down," Max glared at Keith. "That doesn't matter now. What matters is getting somewhere safe. Do either of you have a car?"

Jenny nodded.

The expression on her face looked a lot like how Max felt.

His stomach felt like it was tied in a thousand knots.

"George and I were going to the station," Max continued. "You can come with us if you want, but honestly, I would recommend hitting the bridge inland before I--"

"To answer your question, Keith," George sat up straight, cutting Max short. "Someone did know about this before it happened. The sad thing is, nothing got done about it." The old man reached into his mouth and pulled out the large wad of chew from his mouth. With one flick of the wrist, it hit tile floor with a wet *slap.*

"What are you talking about," Keith said, not once looking down at the chew on the floor. "Who... who knew something?"

George cleared his throat and locked eyes with Max, who was already staring at him. "I did... but not just me. A lot of the elders of Topsail knew. We just didn't want to believe. I can't understand why I wouldn't want to believe. Not after the things I seen as a child. The thing my grandfather done shown me at his lab."

"You mean the museum?"

George nodded.

The others stared intently. A loud thunderous boom reverberated outside.

"My grandfather was a part of the elite scientists that found the book. The book that brought those things to our island. The same book that put some kind of spell on her and sent them all back into the sea. It's just that... I... I never would have guessed in a million years that this was real. I guess a part me always wanted to think it was all make believe."

"Book... what book?" Max leaned forward in his seat glaring at his old neighbor.

"The Necrodine... I think," George said, shifting in his seat. "It's been so long, it's almost like all of it was just a dream. Life times ago."

"I think I heard of that thing," Keith said.

"Yeah, me too." Jenny sniffled, clearly nervous. "It was like some type of urban legend in high school."

"Oh, it's no legend, sweetie." George said. "It's a very real thing. I know, because my grandfather was one of the few men that actually helped decipher the words in that book."

"No way...," Keith said with a hint of excitement.

"Good to know," Max glinted a hit of aggravated sarcasm. "Moved to a town of creeps and my neighbor... my one actual friend on this shitty island is the creepiest of them all. A lying sack of shit!"

"Hey, I never lied to you," George pointed.

"No...," Max said. "No... but you never told me any of that shit. A real friend would have warned about all this asylum poltergeist crap. Instead, you just let us move in. Let Hanna *die*."

"It's not like that, Max." George said, his lips quivering. "It's not like that at all."

"Then what is it like, huh... tell me."

"I thought it was all just my childhood imagination," George insisted. "That my grandfather working at that lab--the things that I seen there-- were just me getting carried away in my head. It wasn't real, but now I know I was wrong. I'm sorry. Had I known, I would have told you to leave. Honest to goodness, Max. Please…"

Max stared long and hard at his old friend and after a moment broke the glare. His eyes shifted to Jenny and then to his hands on the booth table. They were shaking.

George reached into his back pocket, pulled the chew out and found that he was out. The container was empty.

"Well, shit hell fuck." He threw the chew container to the floor. It rattled against the tile for a moment, and then fell silent.

"So, if that book worked back in the day or whatever, think it would work again?"

George nodded at Keith. "Yes, but no one knows where the book it. It was lost or taken. Maybe even hidden away. We *are* talking quite a few years back here."

"Well, wouldn't it stand to reason that the book is still in the museum somewhere?" Jenny said.

"You would think that," George said. "But I just don't see that as a realistic prospect."

"Why not," Max asked.

"Because…," George said. "It just doesn't. Think about it… You got yourself a book that does all kinds a crazy. You gonna just leave it at a museum? That is crazy talk. You would want something like that hidden away. Keep it out of the wrong hands."

"But there is a chance it's there, right?" Keith nodded.

"Yes, I guess so. But honestly… do you know how to read any languages that have been dead for longer than when Christ walked the earth?"

"Well, no…," Keith shrugged.

"That ain't no shit. Of course not," George breathed. "So, even if we did find the book at the museum… which is a one in a million chance, no one knows how to read what might be in the damn thing."

Max cleared his throat. "And how is it you know so damn much?"

"I already told you," George said. "My grandfather. He was involved in the Bumblebee Project."

"Yea, but if it were something like this," Max lifted both hands with distain. "Would it be kept a secret, even from loved ones? We are talking about a world changing situation, right?"

"Yeah," Keith agreed. "Seems kind of like something they would a kept the lid on… Even from you, George."

Keith shrugged.

George nodded, taking no offense. "You're right. But that don't mean nothin'. I was very close to my grandfather. And he shared it all with me. The book. The stuff that science took away from the cold war… and that, that thing." He pointed toward the parking lot. "In the end, I think what killed him was the obsession. But like I done said already… I was a kid then. Looked at it with imaginative eyes. Sure, it was me that spread the rumors around school. Got all the other kids spreading it like it were… how did Keith say? An urban legend. It's not like something like that was hard to do back then. We didn't have TV, the internet, and loud music back then… at least when I was real young. So the stories, the roomers… that was our entertainment as kids then. And that's all it ever was to me, or anyone else. Just stories."

Jenny sighed and grabbed Keith's arm for comfort.

"Regardless," Max said, straight faced. "Childhood stories or not, is there anything… and I mean *anything*, that you can think of that might help us out right now? An aversion to sunlight or salt… something…"

George sat there for a moment in thought, and then shrugged.

"No, I'm afraid I don't."

"You think if we went to that museum," Keith said, "we'd find what we needed to fix this shit?"

"Even if we did," Max said, "I think we should head back to Tatter's to pick him and the kids up and just leave."

George nodded in agreement.

Outside, in the distance, just beyond the parking lot of the diner, a multitude of host driven Topsail citizens lurked in the weather beaten darkness.

SIXTEEN

Tatter held the kids tight.

The house shook violently.

The wind and rain sloshed and whipped with a surge of power so great, for a moment, Tatter thought that the roof was going to tear right off of his home.

However, that wasn't what had him huddled with the two kids in the middle of the bathroom floor. Sure, the weather was getting chaotic, but it was something else. Something beating against the living room door.

It was the stench.

By the time they had made it into the bathroom and closed the door, one of the windows in the living room shattered. Then after a few minutes, it sounded like several other windows throughout the house had done the same. At first, he played it off, giving credit to the winds picking up outside.

However, he knew better than to think that now.

Because now… that same pounding that had been the living room door was now at his bathroom door.

Something was trying to get in.

He looked to the wall next to the tub and was thankful that there was no window. Whatever the hell had gotten into the house, and was now trying like hell to get at him and the kids, had clearly gotten in through the glass.

"Fuck…," he breathed, his left cheek pressed against both of the kids heads.

He held them tight in his arms.

Both of them were crying.

"Sshhh…," he tried to calm. It was no use.

Hell, who was he kidding? He was scared sober. He was more scared than the kids. Because, unlike them… he knew the truth.

The pounding at the bathroom door was relentless.

It sounded wet as the muffled *thumps* slapped over and over against the wood. The doorknob rattled with each smack.

Thoughts of that slimy looking squid thing on the computer coupled with the stories that George, Max, and J.J. had told flooded his mind. His heart pounded.

Tatter closed his eyes and could feel his heart pounding in rhythm with the things trying to get in. He thought of his kids and of his love. He missed them. Holding Peggy and Blake reminded him of a time long forgotten. A time of old when his kids were that young. When they, as pure little children, looked up to him. Expected him to push away the darkness. Admired him for having no fear when it came to looking under the bed. Rewarded him with hugs and kisses when he chased away the dark man that lived in the closet. Only now, he wasn't so brave. He wasn't so strong. In truth, he was scared shitless.

Blake grabbed tighter on Tatter's arm.

Tatter tightened his grip in return.

Blake embraced it.

"Make it stop," Peggy cried, also tightening her grip.

Then it happened.

The house began to groan.

Tatter could feel it shifting. Could feel it vibrating. The walls. The sealing. The floor under his feet. The sound of wood as it stretched with verbal protest. The sound was so loud that, for a moment, it actually drowned out the sound of whatever was beating against the bathroom door.

What the hell is this, he thought, feeling the house shake under its own weight.

His eyes darted around the room. Across from him was the toilet. The sink and the mirror was next to that. The mirror was vibrating so bad that he could hardly make out his own reflection against the shifting shapes of colors.

And then… for just a split second, he saw it.

The closet.

"Kids… listen to me," he said, pulling away from them.

Both Peggy and Blake refused to let go.

He pushed them away anyway.

"I need you two to do something for me, okay?" He stared them in the eyes for a moment, and then realized that they couldn't hear him over the roaring groans of the shaking house. He cleared his throat and spoke louder. "I need you two to do something for me, okay?"

Blake nodded.

"Peggy?"

Peggy wouldn't nod. She wouldn't even take her face away from his arm.

Tatter pulled away from her and stood to his feet in a half crouch. Opening the closet door, he said, "I want the both of you to get in there and hide, okay?"

Blake turned and climbed in.

Tatter grabbed the young boy's sister and shoved her in with him.

"I want the two of you to be as quiet as you can. You got that?" He asked, shoving them against the far wall and tossing stacks of towels over them. "Not a sound. No matter what happens."

After a moment, Blake sniffled. "Okay…"

Tatter felt his heart begin to sink. The kids really were terrified. It hurt him somewhere deep, in that same place that his wife rested, seeing them like this. *It's going to be okay*, he thought while covering the kids with another stack of towels.

"Not a sound," Tatter said.

Satisfied that the kids were covered well enough, he closed the closet door.

When he stood and turned to face the mirror, the sudden sound was ear piercingly loud.

The mirror cracked with a guttural split. The glass exploded outward causing him to shield his eyes. The groaning protest of wood, nails, plaster, and sheetrock peaked at such a high volume that Tatter felt nauseated.

Then it stopped.

A gust of wind suddenly surged around him, the rain pelting down into his bathroom with fierce intensity. Water splashed up around his ankles as the violent rain pelted off the tile floor around him.

Soaked and confused, Tatter looked up.

"MINNNNNEEE…," the rasping voice thrummed through his body so low it was like a sonic boom so thick that it rattled his bones.

Blood ran down Tatter's nose, and for a moment, he felt like his eyes were going to explode. Tears ran down the side of both cheeks. And when he reached up to wipe them away he smeared crimson across the entire length of his forearm.

It wasn't tears.

It was blood running down from the corners of his eyes.

Tatter's vision became a filter of red, and when he looked up, he felt his heart almost stop.

The great Old One reached down into the bathroom with one massive hand.

As Tatter soared through the air, leaving the bathroom, he looked back watching the roofless house become farther and farther away. Rain poured down all around him. The old one squeezed him tight.

Tatter winced, and realized he was nearly twenty stories high, dangling in the night air by only her grip.

The Old One was a cobblestone of rock and ocean floor bonded with the fleshy tissues of decay and rot. Rank bile of sea salt and death wafted over him, burning his lungs.

The thing's countless eyes glared back at him.

He wiggled, trying to break free, but it was useless.

The thing stood, bringing them even higher into the night sky. Its many eyes, all formed from various shapes and sizes, stared back at him.

Tatter quivered in fear.

He could feel her grip getting tighter.

He couldn't breathe.

Just when Tatter thought she was going to squeeze so tight that he would explode in her hand, her mouth began to open. It wasn't the mouth at the base of what could only be her face. No, it was the one that made up the midsection of her torso. The jagged bones stretched as the cavity on her stomach expanded. As it opened, a new rancid odor arose. Tatter's eyes burned as the smell overpowered him.

A long tongue slid around inside the open mouth on her midsection. It was green and puss filled. Goo ran between the sharp serrated teeth and down her belly.

Just when Tatter though that this was the end --he was going to be Welder God minced meat, he just knew it, he was wrong.

A guttural voice bellowed out from within the beast. Its pitch was so low and severe that Tatter's skin ached.

"MIIINNEEE...."

The sonic boom of her voice was too great.

Tatter's top half, the half not nestled within the tight grip of her rock-like fingers, exploded.

Red chunks of meat and skid splashed across her hand, arm, and stomach. The green swollen tongue lapped at the splattered rains of the retired welder with delight.

She sang a thunderous song.

The squid-things making their way into homes, and into bodies, rejoiced with one conjoined high pitched squeal.

Together it sounded like thunder and the scraping screech of grinding gears.

*****

"What the hell was that," Max said.

"Let's get the fuck out of here, man." Keith stood to his feet and grabbed Jenny by the hand.

"I wouldn't go out there just yet," George nodded, pointing toward the door.

The loud, high pitched roar was so loud that it shook the diner. It sounded like it had come from a good distance away, but whatever it was, it was big. Very... very big.

"No offense old man, but fuck you and your stories." Keith flicked him the bird.

The young man took three long striding steps toward the door with Jenny at his side.

"I don't know if I want to go out there, Keith." Jenny tugged at his hand, hesitant to go outside.

After what Max had seen and been through, he knew the feeling all too well and didn't blame her one damn bit.

"No...," Keith resisted her pulling gesture and grabbed the door. "I've had enough. Now let's leave."

He pushed the diner's front door open and the bell chimed.

SEVENTEEN

Amanda was somewhere in the middle of the street, shambling aimlessly in the same direction as countless others, when she heard the bell jingle in the distance.

The thing inside… no, the things… yes, it was plural now. There were more of them. She could feel them growing. Feel them in her belly, expanding. Multiplying. She was their nest. The things inside her became excited at the sudden '*ting, ting, ting'* off in the distance.

With urgency, the things inside--the things forcing her, and everyone around her forward, made her pace quicken. She found herself no longer shambling aimlessly down the dark weather beaten streets of Topsail. Now there was direction. There was purpose.

With a brisker stride, she watched from within the lack of control as she and everyone else around her chased the new sound that had come and gone so quickly.

She wasn't sure how long it had been since she and her girlfriend Shelly had fallen out of their living room window and into the dark rain drenched streets.

In reality, it didn't matter, because this wasn't reality. No, this was a sadistic nightmare. But if she had to guess, it had probably been a few hours at least.

It had to at least been that long.

With all that had already happened, there was no way it hadn't been that long.

Shortly after seeing Shelly fall out of the shattered window of their home, blood covered and face partially eaten, they had both walked. They had all walked. There had been a lot of internal screaming on Amanda's part. But after about thirty minutes of that, she became tired and realized that she was helpless. The things inside of her were going to make her do whatever they wanted. And there was nothing she could do about it. As sad as this thought might have been… at least she wasn't the only one. She was nowhere close to being the only one. Along with her and Shelly, it looked like just about everyone that lived on her block had been dealt the same fate.

As she shambled down their street in the rain, she caught glimpses in her peripheral.

There was Frank and Jill from across the street. They were both in their late fifties and had apparently been married for most of that. They were both true lovers. In a way, Amanda envied that love. She thought she found it with Shelly... but that hadn't been true. At times, Shelly was just as selfish as any of the men that she had ever dated. As she shambled down the street she envied them still. Even in death, or whatever the hell this was, the two lovers shared even this nightmare. Amanda had caught a quick glimpse of the two of them crouched down over someone or something. What they were doing was obvious. What they were doing was the same thing that she had done to Shelly's face in the bedroom. They were feasting. Feeding the things that now lived inside of them. Helping the things inside multiply and grow.

She couldn't be sure, but it was more than likely the very thing that caused her to quit screaming... to give up. Seeing them like that. Not just the neighbor, but all of them. It got her wondering. Questioning whether of not everyone else around her was aware. Was capable of thought as she was, but not actually in control.

She'd actually seen a young woman get chased out of her home and into the streets. She was in her pajamas, much like how Amanda was now, screaming bloody murder and swinging a bat. Internally, Amanda cheered for the woman, hoping that she would get away. But Amanda knew better than to have such high hopes. There were too many of *them* walking the streets now. And that thought made Amanda feel sick. She was one of *them*!

Amanda watched herself give chase with all the others. The woman with the bat was on her back in the grass before she even made it half a block. It hurt Amanda to see the woman die. But in a way she was also thankful of the numbers. There were so many of the 'controlled', as she put it to herself. There were so many 'controlled' on the woman with the baseball bat, feasting, that by the time Amanda got there, the things inside of her must have decided to move on. For that, she was grateful, because that meant that she didn't have to watch herself eat the poor woman alive.

That thought made her cringe even now as the things inside of her urged her toward that faint *ping* of sound. She could feel her body pounding against the earth with each ragged step she took forward. Around her the controlee's numbers had grown into the hundreds. Maybe more. The things inside of her had yet to make her turn and look the way she had come from. This number could only be gauged by the people she could see walking alongside her toward the sound they had heard moments before.

The things in her belly shifted and Amanda's pace quickened.

The diner's parking lot came into view.

When the lightning flashed across her point of vision, the things inside of her shook with excitement, just as they had done toward the woman with the baseball bat.

Someone was standing in the doorway of the diner.

The things inside of her had seen it through her eyes.

Amanda was no longer jogging.

Her body shook; her legs now in full sprint.

She watched with sheer terror as the diner rapidly grew closer.

EIGHTEEN

"Look out!" Jenny screamed!

When Keith looked up, the growing mob was already halfway across the parking lot.

He fell back into the diner, Jenny's yanking arm pulling him back in. As he fell to his ass on the cold tile floor and heard the door slam shut, he could have sworn he saw Amanda, the girl he'd slept with last summer, among the crowd.

As if to prove his assumption correct, the mob of people rushed the front of the diner slamming against the glass that made up the walls and door. She was one of them. In only a wife beater and her underwear, she was covered in blood and soaked to the bone in rain water. She was crazed. Thrashing against the window to get in. They all were. All one hundred plus of them.

"Holy shit," Keith breathed.

"What the hell is wrong with them," Jenny screamed, staggering away from the front of the diner.

"They're gonna break through the glass." George stood from his stool.

"I don't think so," Keith insisted, staggering to his feet as he backed away from the door. "Shatter proof... I think."

"There are so many of them," Max breathed. He was up and huddled with George and the others before he even realized it.

George grabbed him by the arm. "We got to get out a here."

Max didn't reply. He was too shocked by what he was seeing. In a way, he was kind of surprised. Not by what he was seeing, but by the fact that it was affecting him as much was it was. You would think that seeing your wife being eaten by the neighbor, some squids trying to get inside of you, and shooting a few people, would be enough to numb the senses. But this… this was just sensory overload. In a matter of mere seconds, the diner's parking lot was overrun with sprinting lunatics. Within moments of the first body crashing against the entrance to the diner, there were hundreds of them… all pounding against the thick glass, wanting. Blood, mud, and rain water smeared against the storefront's windowpane with each violent fist that pounded against it. The parking lot was no longer visible. It was just a line of bodies, ten, maybe fifteen rows deep and growing.

It was obvious. They wanted in. Each face looked the same. Eyes were wide, and teeth were snarled in a grimace of hungry lunacy.

The pounding fists roared as one.

Max couldn't think.

When George spoke again, he had to raise his voice over the deep rumbling of the windows.

"We've got to go before this place is surrounded."

Max watched his friend's mouth move, and although it looked like he was shouting, he barely made out what had been said.

"That glass ain't gonna hold," George shouted.

"The back door through the kitchen," Keith leaned in.

"I can't," Jenny shrank into Keith's shoulder.

"Well, we can't stay here," he told her, taking her by the hand.

She accepted it and looked like she was about to start crying.

"What the fuck is going on," Keith said.

"I already told you," George nodded, looking toward the door and the multitude trying to get in. He grabbed Max on the shoulder and said, "Max, you with us?"

"Yeah," Max said, shaking his thoughts from the state of disbelief. How could any of this be real? In the movies this stuff didn't just blow out of proportion like this. There was always something slow that led up to this moment. Something that at least gave the characters some type of warning. A head's up ahead of time that helped them cope with the trauma of events that unfolded around them. This wasn't like that at all. One moment, he had been watching cartoons and enjoying the night with his wife. The next, she was dead and the storm that had rolled in had brought with it a morbid squid-thing that turned people into zombies. And these quid things had a mother out there somewhere. This shit just wasn't sinking into his conscious thought. None of it was giving him time to register any of it. How was he supposed to handle this when it was coming at him in waves? Waves that were literally from the sea. Things that were from the ocean... his mind was trailing off again... "Yea... I'm here," he cleared his throat and looked down at the round old man. "What the hell are we waiting for? Let's go!"

They rounded the counter with Keith and Jenny in the lead.

Max's heart ached as he watched them lead the way, hands clasped together.

Just as Max stepped around the counter and into the kitchen area, George right behind him, the so-called shatterproof windowpane between them and the dead outside, splintered.

The *crack* of glass rang across the diner as Max and the others watched the large window split from top to bottom in a wide spider-webbed arch.

Max looked down at George, who was mouthing the word move, as he shoved Max forward.

Max almost tripped to his knees on a rubber floor mat as the round old man heaved him to keep going.

*****

The things inside Amanda's stomach thrived and thrashed with eager anticipation. She could feel them squirm and kick, and although an abomination of thought processes, she found herself wondering how much these feelings might resemble pregnancy. The thought of a small child surfaced in her mind's eye. Her child--inside her kicking and smiling. Just waiting to be born. Warm, pleasurable life. The life that her parents had been hounding her to have… but not before marriage, of course. She thought of a wedding, her mind flashing with images of white. Candles and cake. Of the ring on her finger and how it would feel right… feel natural. These were feelings and images that she knew deep down she would never have with Shelly. But she loved Shelly. She knew the thoughts were wrong, but they were all she could do to keep from watching what was really happening. She tried pushing her thoughts away from Shelly and back to the images of a blissful wedding, but just before they resurfaced, she was shoved hard against the glass by one of the controlled in the crowd.

Her face hit hard against the glass.

Blood splashed across the glass from her left eye.

She watched as the red from her face smeared across the glass.

Reality came rushing back in full force.

The sound of the roaring grunts of those around her. The stench of salt and rotting meat. The thundering sound of the controlled, her included, as they pounded against the glass. There were people inside the store. She had seen them, and the things inside her had seen them, too. The things inside her were hungry. They wanted, needed to feed. And they were going to use her to get what they wanted.

Her vision came back to the surface.

There she was, at the front of the mob, pounding against the splintering glass with bloodied fists.

She could not only see inside the diner, beyond the cracked window, she could also see herself reflected in the window as it shook vigorously against the pounding fists and arms. The left side of her face was covered in crimson, her left eye pressed in from where one of the controlled had pushed her hard against the windowpane.

For the first time all night, Amanda had a new set of thoughts.

Her face... her eye... it was bleeding and sunken in... and yet it did not hurt. She felt no pain. She watched as her knuckles bled. She had been hitting the glass so hard that her hands were bleeding... and she *could not* feel it. But it didn't make sense why she couldn't feel it. It wasn't like she was *dead* or anything... it wasn't like she was...

Amanda screamed long and hard.

The guttural moan that she could hear those around her doing was all that fluttered from her lungs.

*****

The diner's back room was very small.

In essence, all it really turned out to be was a storage area. The narrow walkway that led from one door to another, a door that Jenny said led to the back of the diner, was just wide enough for one person to pass through. On either side of the walkway were various storied goods. To Max's right the wall was lined with rickety wooden shelves. The shelves were lined with an array of canned goods, seasonings, and other dry goods like bread. On the wall opposite that side, the wall was lined with a few smaller shelves. Between these shelves were what looked to be stainless steel freezers or cooling stations. As they passed the coolers, Max guessed that they held things like eggs, milk, butter, and other things of that nature. He shook his head at the thought and moved forward, meeting Jenny and Keith at the back door. Here he was at the end of the world and he was wondering what type of stuff they had in the crappy corner diner's coolers? Wow, he was definitely going to need some mental therapy once all of this was said and done. That was, assuming he was going to get through any of it.

Max stopped behind Jenny.

George bumped into him from behind.

"Why'd we stop?"

"Hear anything," Max asked.

Keith had his ear to the door and held up a hand.

"No, I don't think so," he said. "Kind of hard to hear anything out there with all that moaning and banging."

"Fuck me runnin'," George breathed. "Should a got my guns. Shit…"

"Shh…,"Keith held up a hand.

"I don't hear anything," Jenny whimpered, holding onto Keith's other hand with both of hers.

Max started to say something, but Keith held a finger up, his ear still pressed against the door.

The sudden cacophony of shattering glass flooded their ears from down the narrow hall and back at the front of the building. The moaning grew volumes louder as the sound of a sea of bodies started climbing through the new opening. Max could hear them falling to the floor and getting back up.

"No time!"

George shoved Max forward.

"Go, go, go…" Max yelled.

Keith kicked the door open and all four of them darted through the door just as the first of a massive horde lunged through the narrow hall in pursuit.

George turned and slammed the door shut.

"Where's your car," George said to Jenny, his eyes frantic as he scanned the back lot of the diner.

"Over th--"

Jenny was cut short by the things suddenly slamming against the door they had just exited. She was pointed across the back lot toward a small white car that was parked on the other side of the large metal dumpster.

Just as they all started toward the car, the rain pouring down around them in torrential sheets of grey, the back door to the diner swung open.

The narrow hall helped prevent the massive mob from falling on them in one large number, but it didn't slow them down. In the time that it took Max to get halfway across the back lot there were already more than a dozen of them giving chase at full sprint. He didn't see them. No, there was no time to look back. It was all or nothing. He could hear them. Their footsteps were pounding against the asphalt in their wake.

When Max had almost closed the final leg of distance between him and the white car, he looked up to see Jenny fumbling with her keys to unlock it. Keith was standing at the front passenger door urging her to work faster.

Then… Keith looked up, past Max at the mob. His eyes were wide and his shoulders slackened as he gasped.

Max didn't want to look, but the look on Keith's face made him crane his neck.

When he looked, it was already happening.

George Bradey had failed to keep up.

Two attackers fell on the large man.

Max watched as George fell to his stomach, his forehead crashing with brute force on the concrete. A spray of light brown spewed into the air as the old man's face as it collided with rock and dirt. The two attackers turned into five… and then into seven before George even had time to roll over.

No…

George's screams filled the cold air.

Just like with his wife, all Max was able to do was watch.

The thrashing hands that dug into his neighbor came away in crimson. Streams of intestine and guts clung in their hands. The dead had their feast.

Just when Max thought to step forward and help his friend, he was pulled in reverse by the shoulder.

"Get it!"

The car was in motion before Max even realized that he was on his back and that Keith had pulled him in. The image of George's face bursting upon impact was burned on his retina.

It played on repeat.

George was dead.

Just like Hanna, he had left George behind.

NINETEEN

Amanda cried harder than she had ever cried before, watching helplessly as her body worked against her, feasting on the man at the back lot of the diner. Among the endless rage of gnashing arms and faces, she was there, a member of the controlled that fell on the fleeing man. Her hands dug into the man's torn shirt, past his flayed skin and into his belly. She felt the warmth of his insides and watched as her hands came away red and thick with meaty trails of something... something from *inside...* of him.

She didn't want it. Didn't want to put it in her mouth, but it happened anyway. Her eyes were wide as those around her did the same, feeding that which was inside their bellies. The squid-things were getting what they wanted. She could tell; she could feel it in her.

She cried on the inside as she felt the warm chunks of thick flesh scrape the back of her throat and slide down. The taste was bitter and flat. She cried and screamed, taking more bites. For a moment, she thought that there were real tears falling down her cheeks, but that wasn't true. It was nothing more than the rain that beat against her face.

While she feasted, she had watched from the corner of her eye as the white car sped off away from the parking lot.

The half dozen controlled that hadn't fallen to their knees and started gorging their lives away had given chase. Most sprinted and ran, some falling on the car to then slide off, to only get back up and give chase again. There were others... but not many that shambled a slow grinding walk in the direction that the car had sped off. The ones that staggered at a slow pace looked...well, more dead. Their bodies were a mangled contortion of broken limbs, exposed innards, and many other grotesque things.

Amanda wondered if she would become like one of the slow ones eventually.

She wondered if there would ever be an end to this nightmare.

She cried and ate, then cried some more.

Once there was nothing left of the man they had chased down in the parking lot, most of the controlled that had been eating on his warm body stood and began walking away. The man was now nothing more than a pile of pulp and red sinew that was steadily being washed away by the falling rain. The rain that ran down either side of the parking lot toward different sewage drains was streaked with running red chunks.

She started to do the same.

Then she heard it.

A loud harsh rumble of thunder so loud that the earth beneath her feet quaked.

Lightning flashed.

The bright white that flooded her vision gave a momentary sight to the many things beyond the grey wash of thick rain a few feet in front of her. She could see the large number of controlled around her that had not given chase to the white car… and… and something else. It looked like a mountain in the sky that was moving toward her. But that didn't make any sense. There weren't any mountains in Topsail.

Then the flash was gone, her vision once again narrowed to just a few feet in front of her, the thick rain pelting down around her.

The earth shook beneath Amanda's feet again and this time the mountain came into view despite the heavy rains.

It wasn't a mountain at all.

It was a monster.

The thing hovering over her and the others in the parking lot roared, its voice way up in the sky.

Still, it was loud.

"MYYYY… CHIILLLLDRENNN…"

Amanda's body felt tense against the creature's booming voice.

One of its four massive arms swooped down and scooped up a few of the controlled not even two feet from Amanda. She watched as they soared through the air. The giant thing… ate them!

Oh, my God… no.

With her eyes still focused on the giant monster, something shot up from either side of her vision. It took her a few seconds to realize that it had been her arms. Amanda had her arms in the air as if it prayed. The things inside her stomach were worshiping the giant *thing*. They wanted to be eaten.

This is the end, Amanda thought, watching as the giant scooped up another set of worshiping controlled. *This is the end. My nightmare is finally almost over. Oh, dear God.*

Something fell from the sky and slapped wet at Amanda's feet. The things inside her forced her to look down. It was a hand. Someone's severed hand.

Oh, my God.

A loud thunder rose in the night and the ground quaked again.

The thing, the massive giant had dropped down to its knees in front of Amanda and half a dozen other controlled standing around her, all of them with their hands raised high.

It was hard to really tell what was happening, because the weather was making it hard to see, but Amanda knew. Somehow she knew that it was wrong. The things inside of her were connected, her mind seeing what they saw. Understanding what they understood. Although she couldn't see it beyond the harsh rain, she knew that the puss of acidic sludge that began spraying down was from the giant monster.

Amanda fell to her knees and watched as her hands and arms began to bubble and blister, the putrid liquid coming from the mountain-thing's breasts soaking her from head to toe.

The monster was feeding her children.

With the use of all four hands, the monster squeezed her many breasts, soaking the back parking lot of the diner with rank abomination.

Although it didn't hurt, Amanda saw as her skin began to sizzle and pop with boils. She could feel the pressure beneath her skin as it built up all over her body. The things inside her stomach began to writhe.

Her stomach was building up pressure.

As one, the lingering mob of worshiping controlled burst from the inside out. Leech-like squid splashed out across the parking lot, their undead hosts still with raised arms to the sky.

Amanda's stomach felt lighter... less pressurized.

She could hear the squirming things. Could see them in her peripheral, flapping about on the asphalt. There were just so many of them. Hundreds. Maybe more.

The creature in the sky continued to spray bile from her breasts. The squid-things writhed in it. It was changing them. The rancid puss coming from that giant's tits was making the squid change.

They were growing.

Forming into something else.

Becoming one.

All that Amanda wanted to do more than anything was to just turn and start running... running away from this hellish atrocity. But she couldn't. All she could do was stand there and watch as the multitude of leeches squirmed on the pavement, sliding onto each other and into each other. They were changing... morphing into something bigger. The sound of tearing flesh and slapping skin echoed out across the lot as the metamorphosis took place.

The process seemed to take several minutes, but when it was done, the change was unmistakably different. For every twenty or thirty leeches, that there had been there was now one new creature. Although small, it was still much larger than the leeches had been. Where the leeches had been about the size of a fist, these new things were close to the size of a midget or small child.

In all, there had to be at least a hundred of them.

Their skin was slick with slime, the color grey and clammy like something from the sea. Their arms were thin and narrow. Sharp talons jutted from long mangled fingers. In a way, they still looked like squids because of the half a dozen tentacles that hung down from their narrow faces like long nappy dreaded beards. Their eyes were massive in size compared to their slick grey heads. The tentacles whipped around as if tasting the air.

The mother giant screamed a mammoth roar.

As one, the new beings were off.

It was then that Amanda realized they had wings.

TWENTY

Jenny's white Honda Civic roared down the street at blinding speeds considering the threatening storm outside.

"Slow down," Keith spat, one arm at his side, the other holding the roof as if ready for sudden impact.

Had she heard him, she gave no indication. Her hands stayed firm at ten and two, her knuckles white. Her eyes were wide as if to help see beyond the blankets of rain that pelted the windshield.

Max sat up in his seat and looked out the back window.

Without warning, Max was flung toward the front of the car, the brakes screeching against the slick road. He hit his left shoulder hard on the back of Jenny's seat and then the car was moving again--picking up speed.

"Please, Jenny," Keith said. "You're going to get us killed. Slow down."

"He's right," Max groaned, pulling himself back to a seated position. "There was a tree down on Main at the other side of town. Took up most of the street."

After a moment, the car slowed to a stop.

Calmly, Jenny put it into park. Running her fingers through her hair, she set her palms flat on her lap and stared out the front window.

"Baby…" Keith's voice was soothing as he reached over, touching her arm.

Jenny yelled a high pitched scream of terror so loud that Max thought his ears were going to pop. Her body started to shake and she just kept screaming. Her hair shook on her head as her body shook back and forth in her seat.

Max stole a worried glace at Keith, who returned it, then grabbed his girlfriend by the shoulder.

"Baby, baby… please… calm down. Calm down!"

She just kept shaking and screaming.

Keith slapped Jenny hard across the cheek.

It was unexpected and loud. The sudden *smack* even sent Max back in his seat with disbelief.

With his other hand still on Jenny's shoulder, Keith tried again.

"Baby, calm down." This time his words were like whispers of peace.

It had worked. Jenny was no longer screaming.

Instead, she sat there with wide eyes, the red mark across her cheek setting a rosy red streak on one side of her face.

"Now," Keith whispered. "You are going to get out of the car and trade seats with me, okay?" His words were slow.

Jenny didn't respond.

Keith looked back at Max and nodded. Max wasn't honestly sure what to do, so he just nodded back.

Keith proceeded to open his door. Stepping out into the rain, he rounded the front of the car and opened the driver's side door. Max watched quietly as the man eased his girlfriend out of her seat and began walking her around to the other side. She complied, silent and almost comatose. Max couldn't help but relate. He had felt that way, once, if not twice, tonight. The gravity of it all was just too much for the human mind to take in. He didn't blame her for shutting down. In a way, that was all he really wanted to do. The thought of George being eaten alive fought for supremacy among other terrifying thoughts and it won.

Once Jenny was in place, Keith closed her door and rounded the front of the car once more. He hopped in and slammed the door shut. In the moments of opening and closing the car door, it was amazing to Max how much the closed doors muffled the sound of heavy rain.

It was coming down hard.

"Now," Keith said. "Fuck all this zombie shit. Let's get the fuck out of here. I'm headed to the Surf City bridge and getting as far away as possible. Any objections?"

Jenny didn't reply. Her eyes still held that blank wide gaze.

Max thought of his wife's cold dead body back at the house. She deserved more than to just be left there like that. He needed to get there and take care of her remains. He thought of J.J. driving the streets drunk and how he felt responsible for finding the young officer. And Tatter… Peggy and Blake. He still had Tatter's car. He was obligated to get it back to him. Max pushed that thought aside, realized that it was stupid to be worry about the man's car at a time like this. They could get the car later when all of this was finally over. He thought of George and how he had just abandoned his friend. How he had just let the old man die like that. Hadn't even bothered to help.

"I said, any objections?" Keith asked, putting the car into drive.

"No…," Max breathed, shaken from his thoughts. His voice was soft and distant. "No… the bridge sounds fine."

"Good…"

With that, the car was once again in motion. This time at a less frantic pace. With where they were currently located, the bridge was probably less than five minutes away, even in the current weather conditions.

Max thought to mention the police station idea that he and George were going with and how he needed to report his loss to the proper authorities. But then a thought of all of those people… in the hundreds that had suddenly chased them away from the diner. There would be a lot to report before the night was over.

He glanced out the back window again and saw nothing.

There was no one giving chase.

Where did they all go, he thought. *Surely they would catch up to us eventually.*

The sad thing about that thought was that Max had no idea how right he was.

It was only a matter of time.

*****

The Surf City Bridge was a disaster.

Keith had the car in park. The engine thrummed at a low idle. They sat staring at the tropical storm carnage, the car resting about six car lengths away from the on-ramp that led up the bridge.

With how flooded things had been on their way to the bridge, it was no surprise that they found their one hope out of town in its current condition. With more than three detours as a result of over flooded streets, the car almost dying on them twice, the five minute drive turned out to be more like thirty minutes.

Max's heart sank.

In a way, it was ironic. His heart and the island of Topsail actually had a lot in common.

The entire town was sinking under water.

By Keith's uneducated guess, he said that it was likely that more than half of the island was under at least three feet of water. At first, Max found that hard to believe, but now he knew that possibility to be true.

The bridge was under water.

Had it been one of those bridges that arched high enough for boats to go under, they might have had a chance crossing it. But it wasn't that kind of bridge. It was just a straight shot across. The guard rails on either side of the narrow bridge were barely visible atop the murky water. A few parked cars were parked in random spots along the bridge, all of their tires nonexistent. It was like the water's surface was swallowing them whole, slowly rising inch at a time.

"How the hell are we supposed to cross that?"

"We're not," Max said.

"Turn on the brights," Jenny said, finally out of her emotional slump.

She was still acting a little fuzzy, but Max was glad to see her coming back around.

"They're on already," Keith said, checking the switch.

"I say we try for it," Jenny said.

"Yeah, right."

"You got a better idea?"

A flash of lightning lit of the sky, revealing that one of the cars sunken three deep in water on the bridge had the driver's side door wide open.

"No, I don't have a better idea," Keith barked.

"Well, we have to give it a try… what the hell else is there?" Jenny pointed toward the bridge.

"What the hell do you want me to…"

In the back seat, Max seemed to blank out the sounds around him easily. He could see Keith and Jenny clearly arguing about what to do. But honestly he didn't care. His mind was elsewhere. Here he was in the zombie-monster apocalypse, in a car with two people he really didn't know. The people he cared about were dead. And it was all his fault.

His mind's eye flashed bright. He was no longer in the back seat of this car with these two strangers. Sure, he knew them, but he didn't really *know* them.

Hanna's voice caught his attention. She was laughing in the kitchen. Max climbed out of his recliner and headed into the kitchen to investigate. He hadn't even bothered to notice that he was soaking wet, his clothes drenched from head to toe. His pants legs sloshed with each step he took. When he found Hanna in the kitchen, she was standing there in only her underwear--topless with no bra. She spun around from the sink to great him with a warm embrace.

"What's so funny," he said, hugging her back, tears streaming down his face.

He thought he would never see her again and here he was with her now as if nothing had ever happened.

"Oh, it was nothing," she said with a whimsical inflection. "What's wrong, why are you crying?"

"Nothing, honey… it's nothing." He wiped at his left eye.

His entire face felt wet, but he paid it no attention.

Hanna jumped up, still half-hugging him, and kissed him on the lips. She pulled away, rubbing at her lips.

"Your mustache… it tickles," she said, rubbing at her nose.

"I know, honey, but I'm a mechanic, remember? You do want me to look the part don't you?"

She smiled and hugged him again.

Max embraced her not wanting to ever let her go.

"I won't let anything bad happen to you, honey."

"What? Who the fuck are you talking to," Keith barked. "I ain't your honey."

Max was yanked from his thoughts and found himself once again in the back seat of the Civic. Keith and Jenny were both staring back at him from the front of the car.

"I asked you what you thought we should do and you started talking gibberish, man."

Max looked blankly at them for a moment. If he didn't know any better, Jenny looked scared--of him.

"Where the hell you been man, because it sure as hell hasn't been in the car with us."

"I… I'm sorry," Max ran his fingers through his hair and looked out at the pouring rain from the passenger window. "I… I'm just tired. I've been through a lot tonight, and to be honest, I don't know how much more I can take."

"You look like shit," Jenny said.

"Thanks," Max laughed.

"Well, now that you're back with us," Keith raised a hand toward the bridge. "I was asking… what the hell now? I don't suppose you got a boat, do you?"

"No, I'm afraid I don't."

"I'll get out and swim across there if I have to," Jenny said, her eyes agape with fear. "Those people… they… they were dead."

Max nodded. She definitely had one thing right. He wondered for a moment if seeing all of those people attack them at the diner was enough for Jenny to believe all of the other stuff he and George had told them before getting cut short by the sudden mob. The leeches, the fact that they were coming out of people. The old one and the museum's involvement. That damn book. Realistically, he didn't care if she believed. All he needed to know was that he believed enough right now to be scared shitless. She was scared enough, if not by George's stories, then by the zombies, to go swimming across the Surf City Bridge in the middle of a tropical storm. He looked outside again and wondered what the weather man was saying about it now. Surely Faye had become a Hurricane by now. There was no way it hadn't. The winds were getting out of control. And this rain… if it kept up much longer there would be no island left.

"Do you really think swimming across that is a smart call?" Max asked.

"You got any better ideas?"

"So you think her plan is the way to go then?"

Keith shrugged. "Well, yeah. Sounds a hell of a lot better than waiting for those… *people* to come rushing down our throats again. Last time we got lucky. With roads like they are we're going to get stranded if we try to go anywhere else."

Keith looked left and right as if to prove a point.

Max looked to Jenny. She nodded.

"I don't know," Max said, his mind on the leeches. Those things were from the ocean which meant they thrived in the water. If they were out there now in the drink there would be no way of knowing until it was too late.

"Well, I'm not sticking around to get eaten alive like your buddy, George." Keith turned unbuckling his belt, not even aware that what he had just said hit Max like a slap to the face. "The longer we wait, the less chance we have. Those things... those people were following us. It won't be long before they show up... and then what?"

"We die...," Max breathed.

"Excuse me?"

"If they show up, then we die."

"Man, fuck you," Keith spat. "We don't have time for this shit."

Keith opened the door as if he were about to step out of the car. Rain pressed into the car in waves of grey.

"So ya'll are really going to try swimming across the bridge?"

"What the fuck does it look like, man?" Keith grimaced, his voice just high enough to cover the sound of countless flapping wings amidst the falling rain.

Keith was yanked from the car and disappeared, just like that, the driver's side door still hanging wide open.

TWENTY ONE

Peggy and Blake were still huddled together in the darkness of the damp bathroom closet. It was dark and they were both scared.

The heavy winds and rain sounded so loud against the darkness that they both felt like the storm was right on top of them. It was as if they were no longer in the house. But that wasn't true. They were in the closet.

It had felt like forever since Tatter had left them.

Blake wondered if the old man was ever coming back. The rank stench of rot and putrescence had long ago dissipated, but had left behind a pungent odor.

The slamming and banging at the bathroom door had continued for quite some time after Tatter had put them in the closet, but it was gone now.

Blake wondered for a moment if the bathtub of the toilet were overflowing, because water was staring to run along the floor and was leaking into the closet space. Of all the towels that were still covering him and his sister, the ones from the floor up to the knees were soaked with water. When he reached down to feel the floor, the water was up to his wrist with his palm flat to the floor. It was cold and dank.

"I'm scared," Peggy whimpered.

Blake didn't reply, listening instead to the sounds outside.

He heard nothing.

"Me too."

"When is Tatter coming back?"

I don't know." Blake shifted, the water under them shifting.

"I want Mamma…"

Me too…," Blake started to sob.

He forced himself to silence and listened to the sounds outside.

166

The storm was steady and loud.

Thunder boomed in the distance.

"Me too," he said again, this time squeezing Peggy tightly.

She squeezed him back… and they waited.

TWENTY TWO

Jenny screamed!

One time, when Max had been working on an old Chevy pickup truck for the shop, an accident happened. Not just any kind of accident, but the kind of mistake that could have cost him his life if he hadn't been lucky. Hadn't been standing exactly where he was. Max had been leaned over the engine, the hood propped open. With the motor running, he was looking to see if he could tell what was making the fan belt slip--the fan blade dropping speed every few second, then to rev back to full speed. As he did this, unaware of the wrench in his shirt pocket, the wrench fell into the motor. He had been lucky not to get struck in the face. The second that the fallen tool hit the rotating fan blade, it rattled for a moment and then was gone--zooming past his head in the flash of one single blink. The wrench was just a blur of motion as it soared past his head never to be seen again.

That was how Keith had looked when that thing reached in and snatched him out of his seat.

He was just a blur.

Only, he didn't stay gone.

With Jenny still screaming, Keith's arm slapped against the windshield. But that was just it… the rest of him wasn't attached.

The dismembered limb slapped wet against the windshield in a spray of crimson rain.

"Where did he go?" Jenny screamed.

Max jumped forward in his seat and reached for the driver's side door. It was too far away.

His ears rang as he frantically climbed across the center console and into the driver's seat, Jenny's rasping wail right in his ear.

Panicked, Max closed the door and hit the automatic lock. The simultaneous sound of all four doors locking was anything but assuring. They were trapped in.

"Oh, my God, Keith… what was that?"

"I don't know," Max yelled back, examining the severed arm on the hood. Although the rain had already washed most of it away, some blood still remained on the window.

As if to answer his question, the thing that had undoubtedly snatched Keith from the car and discarded of his arm slammed against the windshield.

Max jumped back; the thing was hideous.

His mind flashed to one of the images he had seen on Tatter's computer.

It had tentacles running down from its swollen head, sharp gangly fingers, and …wings. It darted away and came down again, colliding with the car's thick glass.

"What is it," Jenny screamed, still frantic.

"A god…" Max was surprised at how calm he felt.

"A what?" Jenny whimpered.

It came down again, attacking the car with a loud thud. The car shook but that glass did not break.

Then, without warning, three of the same creatures, all of them roughly the same size, crashed into the car all at once.

Max jumped again and Jenny screamed.

"How many of them are there?"

"I don't know," Max said, studying them.

The creatures scratched at the hood and glass with their claws. One of them scooped up the severed arm, swiped at it with the many tentacles on its face, and then flew off with Keith's arm.

Jenny whimpered and reached out as if to beckon the creature to return what didn't belong to it.

"Keith is dead," Jenny whispered over the sound of the things trying to get at them from outside.

"A lot of people are dead," Max said, turning off the headlights and shutting off the car.

"What are you doing," Jenny grimaced with a loud voice.

"Shhhh," Max said, leaning back and low in his seat.

"If we stay quiet, maybe they'll leave."

"Fuck that," Jenny hissed. "Turn the car back on and get me the fuck out of here."

"And where would you go?" Max asked, the noise of their attackers almost overpowering his calm voice. "I don't know if you noticed, but those things have winds. They'll just follow us."

Jenny stared out the window for a moment.

The car filled with the sound of scraping metal and banding claws. In what stillness that existed between those noises, you could almost hear their beating winds amidst the fall of rain.

Jenny stared to say something, but Max urged her to be quiet.

She leaned back in her seat and cringed at the things outside.

After a few minutes of listening to them punch and scrape against the glass, Max was confident that they wouldn't be able to break through the windshield.

All but one of the creatures fell off, leaning into the window with its face. Its long slender tentacles pressed against the glass. Black slime seeped out, smearing across the window from somewhere behind the lapping tentacles. The tentacles pressed against the glass and began to suck, sticking to the slick surface.

Jenny began to quiver, but Max grabbed her knee and squeezed.

"Shhhh," he said softly.

She nodded, forcing a few of her knuckles into her mouth. She bit down on them and watched.

The creature cried out.

The sound was awful. It was like the call of a dying banshee submerged under water.

The hair on the back of Max's neck stood at the sound, making his skin crawl.

With a loud suction POP, the creature pulled back, its tentacles yanking away from the glass. A film of black goo remained where its face had been. From the looks of it, the goo was so thick that the rain wasn't going to be able to wash it away like it had done with the blood.

The creature flew off, the sound of its wings beating as a dismal reminder to Max that all of this was frighteningly real.

Max wasted a second before pulling his hand away from Jenny's knee.

It was over.

They were gone.

"What the hell was that? What the hell was any of it? What is happening to this town?"

"George called her the old one."

"Who is she? What?" Jenny's panicked eyes scanned the weather-beaten darkness. "I just want to go home."

"With our only way off the island blocked, I have a feeling that we are going to find out."

Max stared past the hood of the car. His vision adjusted enough to the darkness that he could still see the bridge under water.

"Where are we going to go?"

"The only place I know to go for answers," Max breathed.

"Where?" Jenny looked like she was on the verge of emotional chaos.

Max smiled his emotions already over the chaotic hill and on the other side.

Tatter had been right. Max was man type three.

With a widened sadistic grin, Max said "The museum, of course. Don't you know anything?"

"The museum? Why the hell are we going there? We should be trying to leave town."

"Silly little lady," Max cleared his throat, feeling fuzzy inside. "Don't you know anything about bumblebees?"

"What the fuck are you talking about?" Jenny sank into her seat, clearly worried.

Max smiled again.

This time, it was in his eyes.

Max had lost it.

TWENTY THREE

Amanda Potts shambled.

Something was different. Now that those things had burst from within her, she wasn't running. As she moved, her body felt off balance, as if she was just now learning how to walk. The hunger inside of her, that drove her forward, wanted her to run… but she couldn't.

After that giant monster had fed her babies, causing the leeches to form into flying beasts, she and the many other controlled began to shamble on… but toward what?

She felt as if she had been walking forever now.

The rain was heavy against her cold skin.

She was beyond the point of wondering if she would be released from this nightmare. She was beyond wondering if she would die. Because she knew… she was dead. And this was the nightmare of hell after death.

Then, when she was in a lull of depression that would surely be her eternal fate, she heard it.

The call.

The purpose of life, like a gong in her ear--it just rang out clear as day. Somehow, she knew it to be true. Those around her, shambling alongside her aimlessly, heard it too. As one, they lifted their rotting heads and stiffened their stride. The things inside of them were communicating as one. It was on some subconscious level. A level that Amanda couldn't understand, but could feel.

Amanda's mind flashed an image of the mother--her new mother.

She's looking for something… something lost.

But what?

Off in the distance, the giant beast moaned. It sounded like the rattling thunder of the storm.

She's sad.

Amanda's mind flashed a new, familiar image. It was of a stone or something. An egg. It was the mother's baby. The egg was of her seed. It was missing and had been for quite some time.

Amanda remembered seeing that same rock egg somewhere else before, but couldn't quite place it. She could feel the thing inside of her as it probed around in her mind--in her thoughts.

All together, as one, the controlled quickened their pace as one massive shambling pack, Amanda's direction clear.

The mother was in search of her unborn child.

TWENTY FOUR

By the time they got to the museum, the rain had let up a lot. Now it was nothing more than a light drizzle.

That fact made it no less an agonizing fifteen extra minutes getting there. Two of the three streets Max attempted to go down were flooded so bad that he had to turn back and find a different route.

Luckily, the flying things had not followed the car. They must have flown a good distance away by the time Max cranked up Jenny's vehicle and was off. Max didn't say much on the way there, other than the occasional sadistic smile in Jenny's direction.

For the first ten minutes, Jenny had tried pleading with Max. It was not a good idea going there. The museum was practically in the center of town, depending on who you asked. What they needed to do was find a boat and get the hell off the road. Hell, even find a high place to stay dry and out of sight of those *things*… and those *people*.

God, those people were the walking dead.

Jenny gritted her teeth and stared at the building. It was obvious. Max had made up his mind. He was going in, with or without her. She sure as hell wasn't going to stay in the car by herself.

She tried asking him again, for the fifth time since they had parked, why he wanted to go in there. The place was creepy, even during the day. Before she could ask him this time, he was climbing out of the car and jogging toward the front door.

Shit…

Jenny looked in her side mirror and then back at the museum. Max was already halfway to the front door.

"Don't go after him," she said under her breath in an attempt to think of a better plan. "You hardly know Max. And look at him… he has clearly lost his mind."

As if Max had heard her, he turned and waved just as he reached the museum door, the chaotic joker-face smile glued to his mouth.

His expression sent chills down her spine.

She shuddered, looked down, and then back up.

Max was gone.

The museum loomed over her like a rattlesnake ready to strike.

*****

The front door was locked.

Max walked to the side of the building and rounded the corner.

The museum's structure was odd. It sat up on a steep cliff and was a one story red brick structure. It looked too tall to only be one story. The main entrance to the building, the area he had just left, was kept up well. The walkway was lined with a bed of red and yellow flowers, though now they were sunk in the mud by the storm. There was a tall tree fenced in with white that had a black on it for something. Max didn't know what for. He hadn't read it. Hanna had, though. An image of her surfaced as he jogged down the narrow alley.

To his right was the brick building, the windows narrow, but long and tall. To his left was a high wooden fence, also white to match the one that wrapped the tree out front.

Lost stones and gravel crunched under his feet in the alley.

When he reached the end and stepped past the lone trashcan, he was surprised at what he found.

A patrol car was parked at the back of the building with its lights still flashing.

However, that wasn't the main thing he was startled to find.

The back door was standing wide open.

What is this? Max slowly stepped away from the alley and toward the door.

Just as Max reached the door, a uniformed man leaped out of the building.

Max fell back on his ass with one hand covering his face. "Ahhhhh…"

"Fuckin' hell there, buddy," the officer said, his weapon drawn on Max. "'You 'bout gave me a damn heart attack."

He holstered his gun and helped Max to his feet.

"Same here, man."

"Thought for sure we was about to get ambushed again. Fuck me, man. You're lucky I didn't shoot you."

"Ambushed?"

"Yeah, it's a long story," the cop said, looking past Max and beyond the patrol car. "What the hell are you doin' out here anyway?"

Max shrugged.

"Let me guess… long story?"

Max smiled.

"Well shit, man," the cop waved him in. "I was just about to close this door and lock up. My partner and me were kind of hoping to hide out here and wait. Hope for the best, you know."

Max nodded and followed him in.

"Hey, wait for me…" Jenny called out from the side alley.

"Dang, how many of you are there?"

"Just us," Max said.

"Well, come on. No sense in standing around out here. It's not safe out here."

"You can say that again," Jenny breathed.

"Name's Mark Reeve," the cop said, closing the door.

The sound of the deadbolt engaging filled the air.

Mark had a patch over one eye and his short hair was bright blond. Max didn't know him, but had seen him around. He was a hard face to forget. It also looked like the man had a really bad gash on his right arm just below the shoulder. The uniform was torn and bits of mud and blood were caked to the tattered bits of fabric.

Mark locked eyes with Max and then turned his gaze to the room.

Max did the same.

The room they were in looked to be some type of storage space. The walls, although brick outside, were a smooth off white surface. Stacks of boxes lined the wall on one side with a fold out table beside them. Whoever had used the room last must have been using the table to sort through the boxes. A few loose boxes were open and on the table, their contents were scattered across the table's surface. Max didn't know what it was, but it looked to be stuff related to an upcoming exhibit. Nothing he cared to rummage through. It didn't look important at all. What he was here for was the truth. And the truth was going to be in that book that George had mentioned.

"Follow me," Officer Reeve said. "My partner is in the lobby trying to secure the front door. He thinks that if we get attacked, it would be from there. But regardless… once we have it boarded up good, we are going to do the same to the back."

"Your partner," Max asked, his pace matching the uniformed man's.

"Yeah, Griggs Vezquez. He's a little hard around the edges, but he means well. Saved my ass a few times tonight."

Max sighed.

Although Mark had pronounced it differently, he knew the name. That was the one cop on the island that Max couldn't stand. The guy would give an old lady a ticket for being too old if he could get away with it. To him, that cop was the kind of guy that watched *Top Gun* one too many times and thought that was who he was going to be in life.

They walked through a part of the museum that showcased different fossils that had been found indigenous to the region. Bones of small and large fish alike hung to the wall, the blacks beside each one there to tell the viewer what they were viewing.

When they entered the lobby, Griggs was doing exactly what Mark said he would be doing.

The front door that Max had decided was locked had been locked for a reason. Even if he had been able to turn the door handle, the two lobby couches, the stack of chairs, and the bookshelf, would have kept him from getting in.

But Griggs wasn't at the door.

No, he was at the right side of the large lobby trying with all he had to roll a massive round stone across the room toward the door.

"I could use some help," Griggs said, not even bothering to acknowledge the new guests.

The stone that currently had tipped on its side was no longer propped up where it had been the times that Max had visited the museum. Normally, it was against the far corner of the lobby with a golden plaque keeping it in place. This plaque Max had read. It suggested that the large stone had washed up onshore from the ocean floor in 1946. For some reason that date seemed more important than the last time he had been to the museum. Now the plaque was tossed aside on the floor, partially cracked on one corner.

"Name's Max and this is--"

Max was cut short just as he stepped up to help Griggs roll the large rock.

"I don't give a shit who you are, pal. I just want to survive tonight, and if we can do that without you opening your mouth, that would be fine by me."

"*Okay then...*," Max shook his head and then proceeded to help the asshole cop roll the rock across the lobby floor.

The sound of stone as it rattled across the tile floor echoed through the lobby. Between Max, Griggs, and Mark, it was easy going. They had the big rock across the lobby floor in less than a minute.

Jenny stood, shifting her weight, as if eager to help do something.

Shoving the rock one last time, the large bolder was in place pressed against the bookshelf.

Griggs stood straight and took in a deep breath. "I think that should do it."

Max looked on with approval.

"You really think we're safe in here," Jenny asked.

"Heck, yea." Mark kicked the rock hard. "Ain't nothin' getting' through that door."

No one else must have seen it, because they weren't acting like they did, but Max sure as hell saw it.

"What is that all over your shoe?" Max pointed to Mark's boot.

The rock was cracked... and... and leaking a thick black substance a lot like tar. It was pouring out over the officer's shoe.

"Oh, God... what is that smell?" Jenny covered her nose.

"It's the stuff...," Max pointed. "That stuff coming out of the rock."

The lobby was saturated with the permeating stench of death.

TWENTY FIVE

Amanda Potts ached inside.

It was a mother's ache.

Something was wrong and the *thing* controlling her knew. Which mean that *she* knew.

The old one groaned in the night. Her roar was volumes louder than anything Amanda had ever heard or felt in her entire life, alive or dead.

The surge of controlled changed direction.

Amanda wasn't sure where they were all headed, but she was very sure why.

The rain drizzled around her as she walked with the mass of undead islanders. Around her feet, what leech-things hadn't found hosts to grow in and multiply slithered past her at a frantic speed. They slid across the pavement in droves of dozens like a blackish grey streak of moving tar. Overhead, she could hear the beating of many wings, but did not know how many. As she listened, forced to walk like all the others, her mind replayed the atrocious sight of those leeches becoming one and then flying off into the night. Although the thing inside of her wouldn't let her look to the sky, she knew what the sound of beating wings was coming from.

The funny thing was, she was no longer screaming. No longer afraid. It wasn't that she had finally given in or even let go. It was that she had finally found her true purpose in life.

The call... it was inside her now. It was inside her with that leech that pushed each foot forward, one shambling step at a time. It was the calling of knowing the truth. Of knowing real love. She was one with that which was old. Before time.

As one, they moved.

Rigor mortis and rot, her skin was decaying.

And it felt good.

Amanda thought for a moment that she could even feel a smile sliding across her stiffening face.

TWENTY SIX

"What the hell was that?" Jenny's eyes were wide.

The loud rumbling of thunder throbbed so hard that the building shook. It lasted for a moment and then was gone. Only it hadn't sounded like thunder. It sounded more like a roar or a groan.

The smell that had permeated the room still lingered, but was now nothing more than a musty, dry smell. A smell that kind of reminded Max of his attic.

Hanna's yarn art.

"The old one," Max said, looking out with lobby window.

"Fuck," Mark said. "So you seen it, too?"

"No, I haven't," Max said, closing the blind and looking back.

Mark looked scared.

With his hand resting on his holster, he said, "Well, we have." He looked to Griggs and then back at Max.

Max looked over at Griggs, who was sitting on the only chair they hadn't put against the door. He had a shotgun spread across his lap and was cleaning or examining it. Max couldn't tell which. The gruff cop didn't even bother to look up from his weapon at the mention of his name.

"I read about it… my friend…" Max trailed off. "Someone I trust told me about it. That was why we came here. I'm looking for answers. He told me this happened before. And that it was taken care of. If that's true, then there has to be something that can help us. Something that can--"

"Bumblebee," Griggs said.

"What," Mark turned to him.

Without looking up from what he was doing, the shotgun folded across his lap, Griggs said, "You came to the museum because you heard about Operation Bumblebee. Is that right?"

"That's right," Max said after a moment's hesitation.

"Going to save the world, are you?"

"We have to do something…," Max said. "George told me about a book of--"

"Save it for the pity party," Griggs cocked the shotgun, the loud click cutting Max short. "That book ain't in this museum. I know… we looked when we got here. I had the same idea. Thought we would find it. Find something in it to help us. But we can't, because it just ain't here."

"How do you know?"

"How do I know?" Griggs laughed, standing to his feet. He tossed the shotgun over his right shoulder and stepped toward Max, a stiff scowl across his face. "How do I know? Because I fucking looked, that's how. You think we didn't comb this entire place? Well, we did. And it ain't here. And we ran into that monster out there. Not just the people. Or the leeches. That actual monster. The one causing all of this. We saw it… her. It killed half the damn police force in less than three minutes. Took the roof right off and just started eating people like fucking sardines in a can. Mark and me were lucky to even get out of there. The only reason we were lucky was because that monster was busy with the rest of the station. So don't even think about coming in here acting like you got some fresh new ideas on what to do… because you don't."

There was an awkward pause.

Max and Griggs locked eyes.

"I… it's just… we have to do something."

"Do something, he says…," Griggs laughed, pointing at Max and looking to his partner. "We are doing something. We are hiding out and laying low until this shit blows over."

"And what makes you think it will just blow over," Jenny asked, hopeful.

"I heard all them stories just the same as every other kid that grew up on this damn island. I didn't think they were true. But fuck man, after tonight." Mark walked to the window that Max was at and looked out. "I'll believe just about anything. The stories I heard as a kid was that the old one comes every couple hundred years. Something to do with the moon or the stars or something. And when she comes, she is only here for one night. When the sun comes up, she's gone."

"But the storm." Jenny groaned.

"Then we'll just have to wait longer," Griggs said.

"I don't know," Mark said. "The storm is dying off, I think. If we can just sit tight until sun comes up, we'll be okay."

"I don't remember hearing anything like that," Max said.

"Nobody asked you," Griggs gritted his teeth. "I doubt someone like you knows anything."

"What the hell is that supposed to mean?" Max stepped toward Griggs.

"It means we don't like outsiders and you don't know shit!"

"Stop!" Jenny stepped in, preventing Max from getting punched.

"I don't care that I'm not a real local. What I heard, however, was from a *real* local. My friend George didn't say anything about the sun having anything to do with--"

Max was cut short by a loud roar from outside.

This time, it was much closer.

Max's ears rang and for a moment he thought that his eyes were going to explode.

When the noise faded, he realized that he wasn't the only one that felt that way.

Jenny had both hands on her head and Griggs was squeezing the bridge of his nose.

When Mark stepped away from the window, Max saw that his nose was actually bleeding.

The blond officer wiped at it, smearing a thin lining of crimson across the top of his hand.

"Your nose," Jenny said.

"Ahhh, my head." Mark touched his forehead.

"I think she's getting closer," Griggs said, checking his pockets. He pulled out a clip and looked at Max. "You know how to shoot a gun?"

Before Max could reply, the gruff man was handing him a 9mm and two full clips.

"The gun is already loaded. Put these in your pockets," Griggs said. "This is the safety. When you need to reload, press this button and the clip will slide out."

Max nodded.

"What do you mean she's getting closer?" Jenny's eyes went wide again.

The door thumped loud with a violent shake.

Jenny screamed.

"That's what I mean," Griggs said, nodding at his partner and holding the shotgun at the ready.

Mark took his pistol from the holster and nodded back.

Max swallowed hard, eyeing the two police officers. He shoved the two clips in his front pockets and held the gun tight. It wasn't nearly as heavy as the revolver he had pulled out from under the bed at home. The thought of killing his neighbor vibrated in his mind.

At the sound of the lobby door shaking again, he shook the thought away.

"Oh, my God," Jenny screamed, panicking.

"The windows," Mark said.

Everyone looked toward the long narrow windows that lined the wall to their right.

"How do they know we're even in here," Jenny cried.

"I have a feeling that we just happen to be in the way," Max said.

"What makes you say that?" Mark asked.

Max nodded toward the large rock blocking the door, the thick black substance long finished leaking out onto the tile floor.

"If that's true, then we sure did pick the wrong place to lay low."

"Fuck it," Griggs said.

That was when the first window pushed inward.

The sound of shattering glass spilled out across the lobby.

*****

Amanda Potts reached the Museum's front door with a large cluster of other controlled. They were close to it; she could feel it. It was a warm feeling. A feeling that she thought she might never feel again. Alongside the other walkers, her fists pounded against the front door. The entrails of her spilled belly smeared across the door, the open cavity reeking with decay.

With each pounding fist that echoed across the door, she became more and more eager. She wanted it. She wanted to touch it. To open it. The thing inside of her wanted her to want it.

Bodies pressed in around her as a mob of the undead crept up, desiring one and the same.

The rock of substance.

Her baby.

TWENTY SEVEN

"Shit," Griggs spun around.

Two leeches leaped onto the floor from the busted window. Before they even had time to start slithering toward Max and the others, a cluster of mangled, pale hands reached through the window, clawing to get in.

Griggs looked as if he was about to fire the shotgun, but he didn't.

He rushed over, stomping on the two leech-things. They both squawked under his heel.

"We got to keep them from getting in," he said, keeping his stride as he walked over to the busted window.

Pointing the shotgun toward the groping hands, he pulled the trigger.

The shotgun blast boomed across the lobby like a tidal wave of sound.

Max's ears rang.

When the sound faded, the hands in the window were gone--but not for long.

Almost instantly, new rotting pale hands replaced them.

The dead moans filled the lobby from the shattered window.

"They're going to get in!"

"No they're not!"

Another window shattered. This time, five leeches slapped wet onto the cold floor. They slithered fast toward Jenny. She screamed and backed away. Mark jumped forward, stepping on two and firing his pistol seven times. With each loud report, the tile burst into a cloud of dust and liquefied leech guts.

"We're not going to make it," Max breathed, looking at the substance that had leaked out from that big rock. "I think they're here for the rock. I think we should give them what they want."

"Fuck that," Griggs said, shooting off the shotgun again at the same window. "I refuse to let these fucks in here."

"MMMIIIINEEEEE!"

The word reverberated off their bones. Max dropped the pistol; his body and brain hurt so bad.

His vision blurred.

"What the hell was that?" Jenny was on her ass, wiping blood from her nose.

"She's here," Mark shouted. "Quick, get under something!"

It was too late.

With a loud groaning earthquake, the Topsail Beach Museum roof was yanked away.

"GGGIIIIVVEEE MEEEE!"

Officer Mark Reeve was scooped up from the lobby floor before he even had the opportunity to spot a hiding place.

The old one hovered over the exposed lobby like a roaring volcano. Her rocky form was mountainous in shape and size. Max wanted to turn and hide. Wanted to run away.

But he couldn't.

His eyes were fixed on it. The countless eyes glared down at him, two of her mammoth hands resting on the building where the roof had been only moments ago.

One of her hands was shaking about.

That was when Max realized that she had Mark in her hand.

"MINNNNEEEE!" The mouth that was her torso opened up with a roaring groan.

At the same moment that Mark exploded into a raining storm of blood and meaty chunks, Max felt his ears leaking something warm. He reached up to them and each of his hands came away covered in blood.

Sound was gone.

Max couldn't hear.

He could see Jenny on the floor screaming bloody murder as half dozen flying squid-things tore into her, tearing her left arm off, blood splashing across the lobby floor. He could see Griggs aiming the shotgun up at the old one. He could see the shotgun shake in the cop's hand as sparks burst from the barrel, but he heard nothing.

Mist rained down around him.

Griggs dropped the shotgun and ran up to Max, who still had his eyes fixed on the monster overhead.

Griggs shook Max.

When Max looked down, the rugged officer was picking up something from the floor.

The pistol he had dropped.

The old one roared again. Max knew this not because of sound, but because of the vibrations. His body shook with painful velocity. He thought his skin was going to come right off, it felt so bad. Even still, he could not look away.

Then the front wall of the museum came down from the shear weight of the old one's might.

As one, the mob of countless zombies stormed the lobby.

As if in slow motion, Max watched as they shambled toward him, all of them mangled and gore covered. One of them, he even recognized. It was Amanda Potts. He had helped her with her radiator last summer. She was nice even though she tried to lie about her sexuality all the time. It wasn't like no one knew it.

Funny thing was, now as she approached him with that look of hunger in her eye, she *seemed*… happy.

He wasn't sure, but she looked as if she was smiling.

Seeing her happy made a funny feeling rise inside of Max.

He felt happy, too… though he knew he shouldn't.

Just before the zombies reached him, Griggs was overrun and taken down by biting and gnashing teeth, he was soaring through the air. He was probably ten stories up before he even registered that the old one had snagged him up and was now holding him tight.

She squeezed.

The pain… it was too much.

Max embraced it.

Just before all of the blood was forced into his face and his head ruptured like a watermelon under a sledge hammer, he had one thought.

I wonder if they will have lemons in heaven. You can't have tea without any limes.

TWENTY EIGHT

The storm was over the next morning.

The sun rose to a new, beautiful day. Birds chirped and dogs barked happily.

What Mark Reeve, the police officer, had said was true. The Old One and all of her children was gone. Yes, there was plenty left behind as evidence of her visit, but she was gone now, deep in the sea to sleep a little while longer.

Blake and Peggy woke up that morning groggy and confused. They had almost forgotten all about last night and had slept most of the night in the bathroom closet.

Stiff and hungry, Blake shifted, shoving his little sister aside.

She stirred and woke.

When they opened the door, they were amazed to find that the storm had blown away the roof.

"Wow…," Blake said, climbing out of the closet.

Peggy rubbed her eyes and stood to her feet beside her big brother. "Is Mommy home?"

"I don't know," Blake said, eyeing the storm's damage.

"I'm hungry," Peggy whined. "We should go see if Tatter will make us breakfast."

She giggled.

"What's so funny?"

Peggy reached up, and took her brother's hand. "Tatter is a funny name."

Afterwards from the Author

Don't get mad.

I know what you are thinking.

But first, just hear me out. Some of you might think to yourself that the book ended too abruptly, or that I shouldn't have killed off my main characters. Why didn't anyone live?

Well, here is the thing... I have written quite a few survival horror novellas and novels. All of them have a protagonist that, by the end of the story, figures out what to do and saves the day. But let's be realistic. If Cthulhu or any of the other Lovecraftian gods were at your door, do you really think you would make it? I wanted to write a novel that let you think the protagonist was going to save the day, but at the last second, he doesn't. Why did I want to do that? Because I wanted to give my readers something they wouldn't expect. I wanted to change the mold and tell a story where everyone dies. Sure, not everyone died in this book, but still... you get the point. Besides, what better story to do this with than with a Lovecraft homage, right? Although it might not be what you expected at the end, I hope that you enjoyed this story and that it caught you off guard. If it did that, then I am happy as a writer.

The initial idea for this novel was simple. I wanted to write a Lovecraft based story. Honestly, I could have gone in any direction, but I wasn't sure which. So, with that, I came up with a solution. I commissioned Alan M. Clark to do the cover art. I, however did this prior to writing a single word for the book. Why would I do that, you ask? Well, Alan frequently does what he calls dilation exercises. This is where you look at something and become inspired by what you see. When commissioning Alan for this piece, the only guideline that I gave was that the art was to be Lovecraftian in nature. With that, he ran with it. I have to say that I am very happy that I did that, because this cover is freaking awesome! Along with the cover art as a dilation exercise, Alan provided me with a few words on what the painting was to him.

This is what he said:

After an eon of dreaming up mayhem for the sentient toys she so loved and hated, the Old One awoke with a roar, worried that she had pushed chaos too far. Had her latest nightmare, a delightful excursion into a zombie apocalypse, destroyed all human beings or might she find enough survivors tucked away in defensible positions that her collection could be rebuilt and the games continue?

Now, I did not totally run with his concept of what the art represented, but I did run with it. This book is a result of that running.

I hope you enjoyed it.

P. A. Douglas, July 2013

About The Author

P. A. Douglas is the author of several survival horror novels, novellas, and short stories including Watchers, Rancid, and Killer Koala Bears from Another Dimension. His work has been praised by several well-known authors and has appeared in Fangoria Magazine. No longer a nationally touring singer-songwriter, under the name: The Cries Of, Douglas owns and operates a small bizarro press (*Bizarro Pulp Press*). With more than a dozen music related releases and countless national tours under his belt, he has recently decided to give away all of his music for free as digital downloads. Douglas lives in South East Texas.

Visit him at: www.indie-inside.com
Follow him at: www.twitter.com/indie_inside